Murder
IN THE
ORCHARD

BETTY
ROWLANDS

bookouture

Published by Bookouture in 2019

An imprint of StoryFire Ltd.

Carmelite House
50 Victoria Embankment
London EC4Y 0DZ

www.bookouture.com

ISBN: 978-1-78681-873-7
eBook ISBN: 978-1-78681-872-0

CHAPTER ONE

Stewart Miles Haughan (pronounced to rhyme with 'often'), joint proprietor with his wife Verity of the Uphanger Learning Centre in Gloucestershire, reached for the last item in his in-tray. On the other side of the desk sat his secretary, Peggy Drage, her eyes on her notebook and her pencil poised. One couldn't relax for a moment when taking dictation from Stewart. He would grab a letter, scan it briefly, perhaps hurl a couple of questions at her (and bawl her out if she did not have the answers at her fingertips) before the reply came rattling out with the speed of machine-gun fire, impossible to take down verbatim. Not that it mattered unduly if one missed something here and there. Stewart's memory was in some respects as unreliable as his temper; so long as the main thrust of his message came across, the actual wording was of secondary importance. In any case, putting a good letter together was one of the things you paid a secretary for, wasn't it? The only time he made a comment was when something displeased him. Like now.

'What the bloody hell's this?' He leapt to his feet and leaned across the desk, holding a sheet of paper under Peggy's nose. Startled, she looked up and quailed a little at the fury in his expression; this was more than one of his normal tantrums. His voice rose to a bellow. 'Are you deaf, or stupid, or what? I thought I told you not to show me any more of this crap.'

Mechanically, Peggy took the paper and glanced at the three lines typed on it. Oh Lord, not another one! How on earth had it got into his in-tray?

'I didn't put it there,' she said, struggling to keep her poise in the face of his bullying manner. 'I'm sure it didn't come in the post.'

He wouldn't believe her, of course. It was easier to call her a liar and an incompetent fool than to make any sort of rational attempt to find out who was sending these wretched little missives.

'Then bloody well find out where it did come from,' Stewart snarled. He made a throwing movement towards her; had the paper been a more weighty object it would have hit her in the face instead of fluttering into her lap. 'If I see any more of those sheets of arse-paper, you're fired!'

Peggy stood up, gathered the pile of correspondence and returned it to the empty in-tray. 'Stewart, I have absolutely no idea how that thing got in with your mail,' she said firmly. 'Any more than I was able to account for the ones that did come through the post.'

'I suppose you're telling me the fairies are sending them. Little poems, must have been written by the little people!' He grinned unexpectedly, his good humour restored for the moment by his own wit. 'Just make sure I don't see any more of them, that's a good girl.' He reached for the telephone. 'Give me a line.'

The storm had blown itself out. Thankfully, Peggy withdrew to the outer office and connected Stewart's extension to the exchange. Within seconds, he could be heard browbeating some other unfortunate who had failed to meet his expectations. Meanwhile, questioning faces turned in Peggy's direction.

'Another one?' asked Sadie Warner, junior clerk and general dogsbody.

'It was in with his letters. Which of you put it there? Well, one of you must have done,' she continued as both Sadie and the accounts clerk, Pam Sinclair, looked blank and shook their heads.

'George?'

The retired bank employee who came in three days a week to look after the Centre's library of textbooks and cassettes glanced over his shoulder from his seat in the corner and said emphatically, 'Not me.'

Sadie edged forward, her round face alight with eager curiosity. 'What's this one say?'

Everyone clustered round while Pam, craning over Peggy's shoulder, read aloud:

> Spring ended too soon
> With no summer to follow
> Winter is so cold

Martin Morris, the gardener and handyman, who had called in to pick up some car keys and remained to eavesdrop on the latest splenetic outburst from their employer, gave a soft whistle. 'That's creepy,' he remarked. 'Any idea what it means?'

'Haven't a clue,' said Peggy. 'Unless … maybe it's a reference to a nuclear winter …'

'Or the destruction of the rain forests?' suggested Sadie, who was into environmental causes and had recently joined in a demonstration against the use of tropical hardwoods.

'Why send it to Stewart?' said Pam. 'He's the last person to heed cryptic warnings.'

'Perhaps he's got a mahogany toilet seat in his bathroom,' said George drily, without turning round.

Peggy shook her head. 'If that's what's behind it' – the unintentional *double entendre* sent the two girls into a fit of the giggles and earned them a frown of disapproval – 'I mean, if that's the reason for all these messages, then the person sending them obviously doesn't know Stewart. He's not interested in the environment.' Or anything else that doesn't directly concern him, she thought to herself, as she went back to her desk. She was still smarting at the threat of dismissal … not that he meant it, of course, but the suggestion that she might be considered dispensable hurt all the same.

'I reckon he's got *some* idea of what it's all about,' said Martin, jerking his head in the direction of Stewart's office door, behind which yet another hapless individual was taking verbal punishment, 'or he wouldn't have got in such a rage.'

'I doubt it,' said Peggy with a shrug. 'He barely glanced at it before he threw it at me.' She screwed the piece of paper into a ball and dropped it into the bin beside her desk. 'He didn't take much interest in the others, either.'

'How many has he had altogether?' asked Martin.

'Quite a few – at least half a dozen. They've all been on the same sort of melancholy theme, but at the same time whimsical and airy-fairy.' She smiled. 'Maybe that's what made him think the "little people" might have written them. Oh well, better get on with some work. That goes for you lot as well,' she added. Pam and Sadie scuttled back to their desks while Martin, with a departing wave, returned to whatever task he had set himself that morning.

Pounding away at her typewriter – despite repeated requests, Stewart flatly refused to buy a word processor – Peggy asked herself for the hundredth time why she had come to Uphanger. The answer was simple: despite his cavalier treatment in years gone by, she was still in love with him. She had learned to hide her feelings; indeed, there were times when she was able to put them – and the brief affair that had brought her so much grief – from her mind. She was under no illusions about Stewart's attitude; for him, it was something that had never happened. Discarded mistresses and inconvenient promises were all alike to him: forgettable.

Above all things he was a business man, pushy, ruthless and ambitious. He wanted an efficient secretary to help him get Uphanger Learning Centre established in a highly competitive market and had persuaded her to take the job, using all the charm that had seduced her so long ago. Against her better judgement and the advice of those closest to her, she had agreed, happy to think that he needed her. She knew from experience that he was hell to work for, but no matter how much his moods hurt her, life without him would hurt even more. So she put up with his searing comments, his sarcasm and abuse, knowing that they were as ephemeral as his promises.

A preposterous, impossible, infuriating man. She loved him, but there were times when she could murder him.

By half-past four, the classes were over. There followed the usual series of visits from students wishing to exchange books or tapes, check travel arrangements or pick up messages, but now the last car had vanished down the sweeping, gravelled drive and a temporary lull settled over the office. Pam and Sadie had gone off to the ladies' room to powder their noses and discuss plans for the evening; George had already tidied away the returned books and cassettes, and gone home.

Peggy finished the last of the day's letters, checked it and put it in the signature book with the others. As she flipped through the blotting-paper sheets in search of the first free space, her hand froze.

'Oh no, I don't believe it!' she muttered. Tucked between the last two pages was a sheet of paper that she had not put there. Two in one day. This was getting beyond a joke. If Stewart were to see it, he'd blow his top. He'd think …

The door to the inner office was flung open and Stewart breezed out, apparently in an excellent humour. 'Got my mail ready? There's a good girl … what've you got there?'

Peggy's first thought had been to hide the missive, but Stewart's eyes were sharp and any furtive movement would have aroused his immediate suspicion. She screwed it up and tossed it into the bin.

'Just another of those stupid poems,' she said calmly. 'Nothing for you to worry about.'

'Oh, right.' His tone was even, but the air of bonhomie with which he had entered was gone. He took the signature book and retreated, closing the door behind him.

The girls came back, prinked and freshly perfumed, and prepared to leave. Martin called in to return the keys and exchange some friendly banter with Pam whom, it was generally believed, he fancied. Stewart re-emerged, handed over the signed correspondence without comment and stood watching, his hands in his pockets, while the three women, with Martin's willing assistance, folded the letters, sealed and stamped them. The day's work was done and the four of them went outside into the warm September sunshine, exchanged farewells and went on their separate ways.

None thought to glance back through the window of the general office. Had they done so, they would have been puzzled to see Stewart rummaging through the contents of Peggy's litter bin.

CHAPTER TWO

Melissa Craig sat down on the wooden seat outside the cottage adjoining her own and accepted a cup of Earl Grey tea from her friend Iris Ash.

'Just what the doctor ordered,' she said with a grateful smile. 'Gardening is thirsty work.'

Iris, brown as a ripe hazelnut and lean and supple as a willow stem, sat down beside Melissa and squeezed the slice of lemon in her tea with the back of a spoon. 'Ideal weather for it,' she remarked.

It was indeed a perfect September afternoon, mellow, golden and peaceful. The little stone patio where the two women sat was encircled with flowers, every plant chosen as much for its fragrance as its blooms. There was vanilla-scented phlox, aromatic bergamot, old-fashioned tea roses and pinks with their hint of cloves. Beyond the border was Iris's kitchen garden, from which every year she harvested miraculous quantities of the fruit and vegetables that formed an important part of her diet. It was largely due to her influence that Melissa, who had never thought of herself as a gardener until she came to live next door, derived much quiet pleasure and satisfaction – although never such spectacular crops – from her own plot.

Iris finished her tea and put her cup and saucer on a low wooden table, bleached, like the chairs, almost white from constant exposure to the sun, rain and snow of the Cotswolds. She flexed her arms and then clasped her hands behind her head as she surveyed her little kingdom with an air of supreme contentment.

'Friday again,' she remarked. 'Any plans for the weekend?'

Melissa hesitated for a moment before saying, as casually as she could, 'I'm having dinner with Ken Harris tomorrow.'

Iris gave her a keen glance. 'Seeing too much of that policeman,' she said. 'Still a married man, remember. What if the wife comes back?'

'She wants a divorce. Didn't I tell you?'

'Even more tricky. Next thing, he'll be wanting to move in with you.'

'He's already asked me to move in with him,' admitted Melissa.

'Mel! You aren't going to?' Iris's sharp features registered shock and dismay, and her voice held a note of anxiety that Melissa found both gratifying and touching. She put a hand on her friend's shoulder.

'Would you miss me?'

'Course I would.' Iris shook off the hand with an irritable movement. 'Not the point. Drive you mad in a month, living with that man. Any man.'

'I daresay you're right.' Melissa put her empty cup beside Iris's and helped herself to another home-baked cookie. 'In fact, I know you are. I'd have to adapt to his routine – or rather, lack of it – and I'm sure my writing would suffer. And I don't think I could bear the thought of leaving all this.' She made a gesture which encompassed the two cottages, their gardens and the secluded valley in which they lay. As if to add weight to the argument, a robin, perched in the elder tree that gave Iris's cottage its name, suddenly burst into song.

'There you are, then,' said Iris, as if that ended the matter.

'The trouble is, he's so darned persuasive,' Melissa complained. 'Says I can have a free hand in the house, change things round to suit me, rig up the spare room as a study …'

'Hm!' sniffed Iris. 'That's men all over. Wheedle away until they've got you where they want you and then expect you to dance to their tune.' This, for her, was an unusually long speech and gave an indication of the depth of her feelings.

'Don't tell me you're having the same trouble with Jack Hammond?' Iris had recently developed a relationship, the depth and intimacy of which she was careful not to reveal, with a fellow artist who lived in Somerset and whom she visited from time to time. He had not, so far as Melissa was aware, ever been invited to Elder Cottage.

A mischievous gleam shone in Iris's bright grey eyes, giving her the appearance of a benevolent witch. 'Trouble? Not on your life. Knows exactly where he stands. Good pal, Jack,' she added, her expression softening.

Melissa nodded with understanding. Iris had been hurt more than once in the past; no one could blame her for being cautious. It was a lesson she herself would do well to learn. 'As a matter of fact,' she said slowly, 'I've been thinking of going away somewhere quiet for a few days, just to think things over.'

Iris paused in the act of adjusting the tortoiseshell slides that held her short, mouse-brown hair in place and gave a curious stare. 'Quieter than Upper Benbury? You going into retreat?'

'Something like that. Not in a religious house, though. A "writers' retreat". Do you remember that time I was asked to give a week's course in crime fiction at a place near Stowbridge?'

'I remember. Too mean to pay a decent fee, weren't they? Place with an odd name.'

'Uphanger Learning Centre. You're right about the fee. They were only offering peanuts and Joe Martin advised me to turn them down. I heard later on the grapevine that they got a journalist who used to write crime reports for the *Gazette* to run the course. I don't think it was a howling success.'

'Serve 'em right for being stingy. So what's this about a retreat?'

'They've converted a disused stable block into study bedrooms where harassed writers can hide away from it all to work on their masterpieces. Find peace and regain inspiration in the rustic tranquillity of Uphanger – so runs their blurb.'

'You reckon this'd help you sort out Ken Harris?'

'It might not be a bad thing to disappear for a little while.'

'Do an Agatha Christie?' suggested Iris with a grin. 'Make good publicity – your agent would love it.'

'I'm not telling Joe,' said Melissa firmly. 'He's another reason why a few days beyond the reach of a phone would be bliss. He's been on to me twice this week, asking when the next book's going to be finished.'

Iris stood up and put on her gardening gloves. 'Onions have priority today. Let's get the jobs finished.'

'Right. I'll get back to my potatoes. I've only one more row to lift.' Melissa collected the tea things and put them on a tray. 'Shall I take these into the kitchen on my way out?'

'Thanks.' Iris set off down the garden. Halfway along the path she turned. 'Let me know when you decide about going to Up Yours, won't you?'

'Up*hanger*,' corrected Melissa, laughing. 'You'll be the first to know. In fact, you'll be the only one to know.'

CHAPTER THREE

In the kitchen of Uphanger Manor, Verity Haughan was preparing the evening meal. Chicken casserole with rice and green beans. When she was a child, Friday's supper had always been fish – her mother's St Peter's pie had been a legend in the family – but Stewart hated fish so she seldom had it nowadays unless they went out for a meal, something they hadn't done for a long time.

Verity put the casserole in the oven and went over to the window. Immediately outside was the kitchen garden, enclosed by a dry-stone wall which marked the boundary of the manor grounds and beyond which lay a familiar and well-loved landscape of woodland, pasture and arable fields. Under a blue sky flecked with high clouds a tractor, pursued by a flock of eager gulls, was ploughing the stubble of a recently harvested crop. It left a dusty wake that hung in the air like gauze and shimmered in the late afternoon light.

Martin Morris was still at work at the far end of the kitchen garden, lifting potatoes. Verity opened the window and leaned on the sill, watching him. If he should turn round, she would greet him and maybe he would leave his task for a few minutes and stroll over for a chat. Or she could wander out there on the pretext of enjoying the cool evening air after a day spent in her studio.

She found Martin a sympathetic, although reserved, character; during the short time that he had been at Uphanger they had had quite a few conversations, mostly about the garden but occasionally on other topics. As she watched him forking over the soft earth and throwing the smooth, pinkish-white potatoes into a basket, she reflected that although she had spoken to him freely – perhaps a little too freely at times – about herself, he had revealed very little of his own history. Beneath a quiet but friendly exterior he seemed to be a very private person; so far as she was aware he never went out, but spent his free time in the small caravan where he lived in solitude in a secluded corner of the orchard. It was comfortable enough, of course – Verity herself had seen to that – but it seemed unnatural for a comparatively young man to hide himself away. He was supposed to be writing a thesis, but no one knew what it was about. Enquiries about progress never elicited anything but the vague response that it was 'coming along slowly'.

Verity turned from the window and set a pan of water on the stove for the rice before sitting down at the end of the old-fashioned pine-topped table to slice the beans into a colander. Somewhere in the house a door slammed and she heard Stewart approaching. Over the years, since they had come to live at Uphanger, she had learned to use her husband's evening footsteps as a kind of barometer: slow, with pauses to look out of the passage windows, meant he was in a reflective mood, possibly mulling over the details of a new contract: brisk and purposeful suggested that he would enter with his head full of some new scheme, demanding her immediate attention at the expense of whatever else she might be doing: a light, sauntering tread, accompanied by a rather tuneless humming – Verity's favourite, this, but all too rare – indicated a satisfactory day and the possibility of a tolerably relaxed evening.

Today, it was none of these. Pounding footsteps along the passage set the floorboards vibrating and the crockery on the wooden dresser dancing. Even before Stewart burst through the door like a thunderclap, his face flushed and his jaw set, Verity's heart sank. Her own day had gone well and up to now her mood had been buoyant, but suddenly she felt indescribably weary.

'What's wrong?' she asked.

'This.' He thrust two crumpled sheets of paper under her nose, knocking over the colander and scattering beans in all directions. 'Some pea-brain is sending me anonymous messages.'

Verity picked up the first paper and read the three short lines. 'It's hardly a message – more a complaint about the English weather. Where did it come from?'

'How should I know? Some idiot's been shoving them amongst my papers. If I catch him, I'll stuff them down his throat.'

'How many have you had?'

'I don't know, do I? I haven't been keeping them as souvenirs. They started coming by post and I thought it was some rubbish one of the students on a writing course had churned out – though why anyone would expect me to be interested in this sort of crap I can't imagine. Now the bloody things are turning up every five minutes.'

'Have you questioned the staff?'

'Of course I bloody well have. They don't know anything. It could be anyone … people are in and out all the time … students, people delivering stuff …'

'I still don't see why you're so het up.' Verity began retrieving the scattered beans. 'If they're all like this, they're not exactly threatening.' She picked up the second paper. It seemed a lot of fuss about nothing, but if she didn't show a proper interest … She scanned the three short lines; each word was like a knife stabbing at her heart.

> Her blood became ice
> She sleeps in winter's embrace
> Never to awake

'Oh, my God!' Verity covered her face with her hands and burst into tears.

'For Christ's sake, what are you grizzling for?' roared Stewart.

'Tammy!' she gasped. 'Don't you understand, it's about little Tammy!'

'Don't talk such crap. That was years ago – we weren't even living here then.'

Verity fought back her sobs as the pain of loss came rushing back. 'What difference does time make? It's about Tammy, I tell you. What else could it mean?'

'That's what I'd like to know. A fat lot of help you are!'

For the first time in many months, despair at his lack of compassion welled up and would not be contained.

'Haven't you any human feelings at all?' she said brokenly.

'It was just one of those things. You can't go on chucking it in my face for ever.' He broke off as a thought appeared to strike him and his expression became ugly. 'My God!' he rasped. 'I do believe … yes, you wrote this garbage!' He snatched up the two papers and held them a couple of inches from her face with a shaking hand. 'How dare you!'

'Are you out of your mind?' She wiped her eyes in a vain effort to stem the flow of tears. 'How could you think such a thing?'

'Well, did you?'

'No!' She looked up at him beseechingly. 'I swear it, you *must* believe me?'

'If you didn't, who did?'

'How should I know?' Anger at his stony-heartedness began to gain the upper hand over sorrow. He had never tried to comfort her over Tammy's death and had barely grieved, even when it happened. To expect sympathy now, all these years later, was a waste of time. She dried her eyes, checked the rice and tipped the beans into a pan of boiling water. 'If it means so much to you, find out for yourself,' she snapped at him over her shoulder.

'I intend to.' He went to a corner cupboard. 'What I need now is a drink.' He grabbed a bottle of whisky and a glass and poured himself a generous tot. He tossed it back neat and poured another, then held the bottle in front of his wife. 'Want one?'

Verity shook her head. She was calmer now, but for the moment she could not bring herself to talk to him.

'Suit yourself.' Stewart returned the whisky to the cupboard and sat down at the table. 'What's for dinner?'

'Chicken casserole.'

'Fine.' He sipped the second drink more slowly, staring out of the window. Verity glanced out as well and was relieved to see that Martin had finished lifting the row of potatoes and disappeared. She would not have liked him to overhear those bitter exchanges.

'I've been thinking,' said Stewart, downing the last of the whisky. 'Some bugger's obviously doing this to wind me up. A war of nerves, that's what it is. Who'd want to do that, I wonder?' He was talking to himself now, frowning, fiddling with the empty glass. 'A competitor, most likely. Someone I beat to a contract, maybe. What do you think?'

His eyes swivelled, focusing on Verity. Their expression was hard and vindictive; she wondered what had become of the romantic young suitor with whom she had once believed herself in love. He had quickly revealed himself to be self-centred beyond belief, almost, she felt in her bleakest moments, to the point of being psychopathic. Was he becoming paranoid as well?

'Well?' he said impatiently. 'Don't stand there gawping, say something.'

'How should I know? You'll have to question the people in the office again.'

'I'm not going to let underlings get the idea that it's seriously getting to me. I'll handle this in my own way, make my own enquiries. Listen to me, will you?'

She was at the sink with her back to him, draining the beans. 'I am listening,' she said without turning round. 'I take it you want your dinner?'

'Too bloody right. How much longer do I have to wait?'

'I'm just about to dish up. You were saying?'

'It's an offence to send anonymous letters, isn't it?'

'It depends.' She put a plate of food in front of him and he began to eat, hungrily, without comment. She sat down opposite him and began toying with a piece of chicken. 'It's certainly an offence to send poison pen letters, or try to blackmail someone, but these are nothing like that.'

'Hm.' For a while, they ate in silence. Then he said, 'This is probably the beginning of a campaign. Like I said, a war of nerves. Well, I'll teach the bastard not to tangle with Stewart Haughan. I'll give him bloody poetry! Got any more of that chicken?'

'You have to find him first,' said Verity as she ladled out more casserole. 'How are you going to do that, if you don't want to involve the office staff?'

'I'll have to think about it. A private investigator, maybe. No, they cost money. I could try the police. Yes, why not?' He gave a triumphant smile, as if the problem had suddenly been resolved. 'It's what we pay our taxes for, isn't it? I'll report it to the police.'

Verity shrugged, waited for him to finish and served the dessert. She doubted whether the police would be interested in such a trivial matter, but there was no point in saying anything. He never listened to her opinion unless it confirmed his own. Let him find out for himself.

CHAPTER FOUR

On the occasion of her first meeting with Detective Chief Inspector Kenneth Harris, Melissa Craig (known to her fans as the best-selling crime writer Mel Craig) had been exhausted, dishevelled and in deep shock after finding the body of a local farmer in a stream a short distance from her home. Harris's attitude at the time had been none too cordial and she had not felt him to be a particularly sympathetic character, but as time passed and she came to know him better, she learned that behind his brusque manner and somewhat unprepossessing appearance (eyes on the small side, lumpy features and a tendency to excess weight) was an intelligent and sensitive man with whom she had much in common. Gradually, their relationship had become closer and more intimate; a short while ago, it had crossed the boundary of friendship into something more volatile, more exciting – and far less easy to handle. As Harris himself, with a characteristic touch of wry humour, had expressed it, sex had reared its lovely head, bringing wonderful moments of passion … and some fierce arguments. They were arguing now.

'Why won't you let me stay the night?' he grumbled. 'No one will know except Iris, and she won't go spreading it around the village.'

'That's not the point. Early morning is my time for working, and I don't want you around demanding breakfast and cups of coffee.'

'Tomorrow's Sunday.'

'So what? My muse burns just as brightly on the Sabbath as any other day. So, on your bike, Ken Harris!'

Melissa got up and put on her dressing gown. She caught a glimpse of herself in the wardrobe mirror and felt heartened at what she saw. With her chestnut hair tumbling round her shoulders, clear, unlined skin and fresh colouring, at forty-seven she knew she could pass for a woman ten years younger – and secretly rejoiced in the knowledge. She turned to glance at Harris, thinking how much better he looked since she'd persuaded him to lose weight.

'I promise not to disturb you,' he was saying.

'Forget it. A three-foot bed is just about okay for making love, but not for sleeping – especially when one partner takes up two thirds of it.'

'Come and live with me and I'll buy you a king-size bed.'

'Don't start that again.'

'You only want me for my body. Well, it's all yours.' He sat up and made a grab at her, but she eluded him.

'And you only want me there to cook and clean and do your washing,' she retorted.

His expression became earnest. 'Not true. I care for you, Mel. Really care. I want to look after you all the time.'

'I know,' she said gently. She bent to give him a kiss. 'And I care too. Only … I've got used to my independence … and I love Hawthorn Cottage and my way of life here … I'm not ready to give it all up. Not yet, anyway, so let's not talk about it any more.' She straightened up. 'I'll go and make some tea while you get dressed.'

Resignedly, he reached for his clothes. 'I suppose I can take some comfort from "not yet",' he sighed.

A few minutes later he joined her in the kitchen and sat down while she brewed tea and set out cups and saucers. His eye fell on a brochure lying on the table and he picked it up. 'Where did you get this?'

'What's that? Oh, the bumf from Uphanger Learning Centre … it came through the post. I very nearly gave one of my creative writing courses there a while ago, but they were too mean to cough up a reasonable fee.'

'What sort of an outfit is it?'

'According to one of my colleagues at Stowbridge Tech, a bit of a bucket shop. The principal is a man called Stewart Haughan who claims to have devised some brilliant new system for language learning. It's something to do with combining traditional instruction and teaching a manual skill like pottery or weaving. He calls it the Creativity Assisted Language Learning System – CRALLS. Iris says it sounds like a sea-sickness remedy.' Melissa glanced up from pouring milk into the teacups. 'What's your interest? Thinking of brushing up your embroidery?'

'Haughan called at the station this morning, asking – no, demanding, I should say, he's an aggressive sort of character – to see a senior CID officer. I gave him Sergeant Waters and I understand he wasn't best pleased at being put off with anyone less exalted than a superintendent.'

'What did he want?'

'Seems to think someone's waging a hate campaign against him – in the form of poems, would you believe.'

Melissa handed him a cup of tea and pushed the sugar basin across the table. 'What sort of poems?'

'Very short ones, I gather. He brought a couple along to show us, but Waters thought they seemed pretty innocuous. A bit dreary, he said, more like some sort of lament … certainly not threatening.'

'Haughan must think they are, or he wouldn't have gone to the police.'

'He said something about a business rival wanting to get back at him for having snitched a contract to give language lessons to employees of some company or other. He wouldn't name names and Waters was pretty sure he was holding something back, but he couldn't get anything concrete out of him.'

'So what does he expect you to do?'

'Unmask the perpetrator, of course!' Harris emptied his cup and held it out for a refill. 'Waters told him politely that without more information – or unless the messages became overtly threatening – it was hardly a police matter, and he went off in the highest possible dudgeon.' Harris gave a gravelly chuckle; evidently, Waters's account of the interview had been a lively one.

Melissa was intrigued. Her crime-writer's mind was already speculating on possibilities for a plot. 'I don't suppose Sergeant Waters told you what was in the poems?'

Harris put down his cup and began fumbling in his pocket. 'As a matter of fact, I've just remembered, he gave them to me to ask me what I made of them. I was just leaving, so I took them away to read later and then forgot all about them.' He fished out two small sheets of paper and unfolded them. He read them, frowning, and then pushed them across the table. 'What do you make of them?'

Melissa read the two short stanzas, then re-read them aloud, counting on her fingers. 'I think they might be haiku,' she told him.

'Hi … what?'

'Haiku.' She spelled it out. 'It's a Japanese verse form. Haiku poems have to conform to a strict syllable count – five, seven, five. Like these.'

'And what do they mean?'

'I read somewhere that they're supposed to "capture a fleeting moment of beauty, wonder or sadness". There's almost always a reference to the seasons, as there is in these. There's certainly sadness. They seem to be a lament for someone who died young … a girl, since there's a reference to "she". I wonder why Haughan thinks there's a connection with a business deal.'

'Maybe a disgruntled competitor shot the employee who failed to get the contract,' suggested Harris with a grin.

'And someone who loved her is trying to lay the blame at Haughan's door. Could be.' She put the two pieces of paper on the table and leaned on her elbows as if trying to extract some deeper meaning from the words. In fact, she was memorising them.

'That wasn't a serious suggestion,' said Harris, a trifle impatiently. He held out a hand for the papers and, a little reluctantly, she handed them over. 'I'd better be on my way.'

The minute he had gone, she wrote the verses down. There was certainly a mystery here … surely Haughan would not have gone to the police unless he believed them to carry a deeper, more sinister significance. The fact that he had declined to give a reason for his belief intensified her curiosity. Suddenly, the prospect of spending a week in a so-called 'writer's retreat' at Uphanger Learning Centre had become very alluring.

CHAPTER FIVE

The Gloucestershire hamlet of Uphanger is reached by a road that snakes around the contours of wooded hills before emerging among open fields that slope away towards the market town of Stowbridge to the east and the county boundary with Wiltshire to the south. Its manor house, parts of which date from the fourteenth century, stands on a rise a short distance from the road, with an uninterrupted view across the countryside. Its elevated position, with lesser dwellings clustered round its encircling wall like children clinging to their mother's skirts, seemed to Melissa to give it a protective, but at the same time a proprietary air. The thought occurred to her that, in theory at any rate, there was something to be said for the feudal system. Pay your tithe to your manorial lord and he will watch over you, provide you with a modest homestead and generally relieve you of all responsibility. Unfortunately, medieval lords of the manor being what they were, the arrangement seldom worked to anyone's advantage but their own. As she slowed down at the entrance, with its imposing wrought-iron gates, she wondered what the earlier inhabitants of the now gentrified cottages would make of the lifestyle of their present owners.

A dark green notice board with white lettering informed her that she had arrived at the Uphanger Learning Centre. The gates stood open; she swung the wheel, bumped across the cattle-grid that protected the grounds against stray farm animals or wild deer and drove slowly up the gravelled drive.

The prospect was a charming one. The house, facing almost due south, was an architectural gem of weathered stone with a gabled elevation, brick chimneys like sticks of barley-sugar and tall mullioned windows. The drive, lined on either side with chestnut trees, ended in a wide, semi-circular courtyard ringed with bright flower-beds. At the top, a sign painted in the same colours as the one at the entrance directed visitors to a car park tucked away behind a beech hedge which, like the trees, was already flecked with the gold of early autumn.

Melissa parked her elderly Golf beside a line of other cars and returned to the front of the building, where yet another notice read 'Reception. Please Enter'. She raised the massive iron latch, pushed open the studded oak door and found herself in a large, lofty hall. To her right was an open archway, through which she could see a wooden counter and a small general office.

As she closed the door gently behind her she heard a man's voice, muffled but raised in what sounded like anger. She hesitated, unwilling to cause embarrassment by appearing at a delicate moment. Then the shouting stopped and a door opened and closed. She waited another moment or two and then approached.

Beyond the counter stood a man and a woman, one on either side of a desk. Their heads were turned towards a door in the far corner of the office; the woman held a plastic tray full of papers in one hand and her attitude suggested that she had just emerged from the room where the shouting had taken place. Both she and her companion seemed unaware of Melissa's presence.

'Well, well, we *are* in a mood this morning. It must be all these anonymous billets-doux we're getting,' the man was saying. His tone suggested that he was not displeased at the thought.

'I can't think why,' the woman replied. 'There's nothing in the ones I've seen to cause that sort of reaction. There must be some hidden meaning, I suppose.'

The man turned his head to look at her, showing his profile. He was tall and spare, with thinning grey hair; Melissa judged his age to be about sixty. Halfway down his pointed nose he wore glasses with heavy frames that looked disproportionately large for his sharp features. His mouth was twisted in a sardonic smile and he jerked his head towards the closed door in the corner.

'*We* don't know what it's all about, but I suspect *he* does,' he said, meaningly.

The woman frowned. She was considerably younger than her colleague, on the plump side, with straight dark hair brushed back from a pale, Pre-Raphaelite face. 'Come to think of it,' she said slowly, 'the latest one was different – it hinted at the death of someone, a woman.'

'I don't remember that.'

'I chucked it in the bin. He never even read it.'

'The death of a woman,' the man mused. 'Could it have been referring to the girl you told me about, the one who used to work here, the one who died … Kate somebody? You said how upset she used to get over his tantrums.'

Melissa was beginning to feel uncomfortable. This conversation, carried on in clear but quiet voices, was not intended to be overheard. She ought to creep away and then return, making sufficient noise to alert them to her presence, but it seemed highly probable that what she was hearing was connected to the mysterious messages DCI Harris had told her about. Native curiosity did battle over the ethics of eavesdropping, but her dilemma was resolved by the sudden appearance behind her of a second woman carrying a tray of china mugs, a jug of milk and a pot of coffee. She wished Melissa a pleasant 'Good morning' and placed the tray on the counter before opening a hinged flap and walking round behind it. The others abruptly stopped talking and sat down at their desks.

'Can I help you?' said the newcomer.

'I'm here for a week's "writer's retreat",' Melissa explained. 'I arranged it with Mr Haughan over the telephone last Monday and he sent me this letter of confirmation. My name's Mel Craig.'

The young woman glanced briefly at the letter Melissa held out and her smile lost its impersonal quality and became warm and friendly. 'How nice to meet you, Ms Craig! I just love your books – in fact, we're all fans of yours here, aren't we, Peggy? My name's Pam Sinclair, by the way, and this is Peggy Drage, Mr Haughan's secretary …'

'"Personal Assistant",' corrected the grey-haired man 'That's what she is, and that's how he,' – the speaker jerked his head in the direction of the door in the far corner – 'refers to her when he wants to impress people. Like he talks about Pam as "my accountant", but he treats her like a junior clerk.' He fixed Melissa with a fierce stare that seemed to demand a response.

'Why would he do that?' she said, feeling somewhat at a loss. The atmosphere had an edge that made her ill at ease, despite the warmth of Pam's greeting.

The man gave a sniff. 'Secretaries and clerks come cheaper than PAs and accountants,' he said drily.

'Oh, let it go, George,' said Peggy tartly. She pushed back her chair and stood up. 'I'll tell Mr Haughan you're here, Ms Craig. He particularly asked to be told as soon as you arrived.' She went over to the corner and tapped – a little timidly, it seemed to Melissa – on the door. A voice barked 'Come in!' and she opened it and disappeared inside. Moments later, it was flung open and Stewart Haughan emerged.

His height and build were little more than average, but he gave the impression of a powerful, dominating personality, backed up by a latent aggressiveness, that made him appear larger than he was. He advanced towards Melissa, smiling broadly, and thrust his right hand across the counter. 'Mel Craig – welcome to Uphanger! This is indeed a pleasure … and an honour!'

'How do you do, Mr Haughan,' she replied. His hand was cold and a trifle clammy. It might have been her imagination, but there seemed to be a lack of spontaneity in his manner, as if he had hyped himself up to give a performance. The flashing smile that revealed a set of very large, very even teeth, did not reach his round, greenish eyes.

'Please, call me Stewart. We're all on first name terms here, aren't we?' He glanced round for confirmation and the others smiled obediently and nodded. 'You've met my staff, I take it? Right, come with me and I'll show you round the place and then take you to the guest wing.' He came out from behind the counter, letting the flap fall with a crash. Over his shoulder, Melissa saw Pam roll her eyes towards the ceiling.

The 'guest wing', when they eventually reached it, proved to be a converted stable block, built originally in the days when horses had exceptionally spacious quarters while their grooms lived in more spartan conditions overhead. Four loose-boxes had been fitted out as studio-style apartments, each with a sitting-room and a small but well-equipped bathroom on the ground floor and a sleeping area, reached by an open-tread wooden staircase, on an entresol at the rear. Stewart Haughan, with a laboured attempt at humour, referred to the rooms as 'cells' to emphasise the monastic concept of a 'Writer's Retreat'.

'You needn't see another soul all day except at meal-times,' he explained as he handed Melissa her key. 'Total P and Q, that's what I'm told you writers need, and here you have it. By the way,' he added, almost as an afterthought on leaving, 'you'll normally be eating in the guests' dining-room – you remember where that is, don't you? – but as you're on your own until tomorrow we, my wife and I that is, would like you to have dinner with us this evening.'

'That's very kind of you,' said Melissa politely.

'Fine. I'll leave you to settle in.' He gave a jaunty wave and departed.

Thankful to be on her own at last – Stewart had insisted on demonstrating every feature of the room as if he were an estate agent trying to make a sale and it had been hard work finding a suitable range of appreciative comments – Melissa unpacked, set up her portable word processor on the desk, filled and plugged in the electric kettle (Stewart had stressed the tea-and coffee-making facilities, as if he personally had conceived the idea) and made a cup of coffee. Then she sat down and pondered her reasons for being here.

Giving herself time to think over her relationship with Kenneth Harris was the main one, of course. A week on her own, without so much as a phone call from him, might prove something – although, she reflected, she was paying what she considered an inflated fee for the experiment. It would also be an advantage to work on her current book without any interruptions, despite being well ahead of schedule and not anticipating any serious problems.

Then there was the intriguing matter of the anonymous haiku poems. The more she thought about them, the more she saw possibilities for a plot for a mystery novel. During her stay, she might uncover some details that would be useful in developing the story. Relaxing in an armchair as she drank her coffee, she was letting her mind run over some possibilities when she became aware of a movement outside the window. She looked up to see a man staring in at her, his hand cupped round his eyes and his face pressed against the glass.

CHAPTER SIX

Melissa leapt to her feet and wrenched open the door.

'What the hell do you think you're doing?' she demanded.

He was a youngish man, bearded and tanned, wearing an open-necked shirt with a frayed collar and rolled-up sleeves, stained corduroy trousers and heavy boots. He looked startled and embarrassed at Melissa's sudden appearance but did not, as she had half expected, make a bolt for it. Instead, he replied in a cultured voice, 'I do beg your pardon. I noticed the blind had been moved … I'm sorry if I frightened you.'

'You didn't frighten me,' said Melissa shortly. 'I don't like being spied on, that's all.'

'I assure you, I wasn't spying. Some suspicious-looking characters have been seen in the neighbourhood lately and no one told me we had a guest.'

'You should have knocked.'

'You're right, I should. Please forgive me.'

'No harm done. Who are you, by the way?'

'Martin Morris. I'm the gardener and handyman round here.'

'Melissa Craig.' Mollified, she held out a hand, but he gave a rueful smile and shook his head as he displayed his own grimy fingers.

'Better not,' he apologised. 'I've been servicing the mower. You must be Mel Craig, the writer?' Melissa smiled and nodded. Despite the dirt and the rough clothes, his speech and manner were more like those of a professional than a manual worker. 'Ah, now I understand,' he went on. 'I heard you were coming, but I thought it was tomorrow.'

'I believe someone else is coming tomorrow.'

'Oh, right.' He half turned away, hesitated, and swung round again. 'You needn't worry about being disturbed. I've been told to keep away from here while there are "writers in retreat".'

Melissa thought she detected a trace of irony in the way he pronounced the final words, but she merely said, 'Don't worry, you won't disturb me,' and was on the point of going back inside when he took a step towards her, looking her straight in the eye. She thought he looked tense and a little anxious.

'That is what you're here for, isn't it? To write, I mean … in peace, without interruption … that sort of thing?'

'Why else would I be here?' she asked curiously.

'Oh, no reason. I just wondered.'

'Is there something odd going on?'

This time he did not meet her eye. 'What do you mean?' he asked, in a tone that sounded a little too casual to be natural.

'I overheard a snatch of conversation when I arrived that suggested someone was receiving anonymous messages.'

'Oh, that. Someone's been playing tricks on Stewart Haughan, that's all. He's really riled about it.' Martin gave an odd half-smile. 'Not that it takes much to wind him up.'

'Yes, I got the impression he's a pretty volatile character.'

'You can say that again. Well, I must get back to work.' For the second time, he started to move away, but Melissa had one more question.

'Do you happen to know anything about a girl named Kate who used to work here?'

He stopped short, but did not turn his head.

'I've heard of her. It was before my time here,' he said, and strode away.

*

At half-past seven, Melissa strolled across what had once been the stable yard but was now a neatly gravelled area dotted with beds of geraniums. At some time in the past, it appeared, an extra, L-shaped wing had been added to the rear of the main house, but in a less ornate style than the original, possibly to accommodate servants. It was here that the Haughans had their private quarters. The warm glow of the setting sun on the mellow stone gave the place a welcoming, homely appearance, in marked contrast to the magnificence of the main entrance. A climbing rose, still covered in fragrant pink blooms, was trained on the wall; mauve petunias and blue lobelia spilled from a hanging basket beside the white-painted door.

Melissa pressed the brass bellpush. There was a brief pause before she heard the sound of footsteps and Stewart Haughan opened the door. He greeted her in the same hearty manner as before and ushered her along a passage and into a spacious kitchen-cum-living room where a slight, pale woman in a loose dress that matched her smoke-blue eyes, with straight blonde hair cut in a little-girl fringe, was stirring something on the stove.

'My wife, Verity,' said Stewart. 'Verry, this is Mel Craig who writes those exciting murder mysteries.'

Verity put down her wooden spoon and held out a hand. She had long, tapering fingers which felt cool to the touch, despite the warmth from the stove.

'I'm so glad to meet you,' she said in a low, but clear and musical voice. 'I hope you don't mind eating in the kitchen – we live in here most of the time.'

'I'm not surprised,' said Melissa. 'It's very cosy … and what a lovely view of the garden. Mr Morris certainly knows his stuff.'

'You've met Martin?' said Stewart. Melissa explained and he nodded in approval. 'Good man, keeps his eyes open. Lives in a caravan in the orchard – you'll see him around. He should have been told you were coming, though. I must tell Peggy off about that in the morning.'

'Why blame Peggy?' said Verity. 'You could have told him yourself – you have more contact with him than she does.'

'It's her job to see to details like that,' Stewart said curtly. He went over to the dresser. 'How about a drink, Melissa?'

'Thank you. A dry sherry if you have one, please.'

'Of course. You name it, we've got it.' He poured two glasses and handed one to Melissa, his air of good humour restored. 'Yours is on the table, Verry. Is the wine open?' His wife, still busy at the stove, said 'Yes' without turning round. He gave himself a generous shot of Scotch and turned back to Melissa. 'You like the room, then?'

'It's lovely,' she replied warmly.

It was a beautifully proportioned room, with exposed beams in the ceiling and mullioned windows on two sides. Modern kitchen equipment and units had been skilfully combined with some well-preserved antique pieces to produce a very satisfying blend of old and new. There were colourful rugs on the floor, a brick chimney-breast housing a modern cooker at one end and two comfortable-looking armchairs, upholstered to match the curtains, at the other. Between the chairs was a low table, on which stood a container of fresh flowers, expertly arranged.

'You should have seen it when we first took the place over,' Stewart said smugly. 'A real pigsty, wasn't it, Verry? I had it completely gutted and refitted to my own design. I'll bet you thought it was done by an expert, eh?'

'It looks very professional,' Melissa declared, affecting not to notice the lack of response from her hostess, or the strange look she gave her husband as she put on a pair of padded mitts to remove a dish from the oven.

'I hope you like steak and kidney pie, Melissa,' she said.

'It's one of my favourites,' Melissa assured her, sniffing appreciatively. 'That smells wonderful.'

'Come and sit down,' said Stewart, pulling out a chair for his guest before seating himself at the head of the long wooden table, one end of which was laid with three places. While Verity brought plates and dishes of vegetables and served the food, he poured wine and drank copiously himself, all the while keeping up a running monologue about his business experience, the establishment of the Centre and the alterations and improvements he had carried out since taking over the property five years previously. 'Of course, it's been in the family for a couple of hundred years, but it got a bit run down towards the end of Uncle Joshua's reign.'

'Uncle Joshua was a very sick old man,' said Verity. It was the first time she had spoken since serving the first course, and there was a wistful note in her voice as she added, 'He kept it immaculate for many years – he loved the place.'

'I wonder what he'd have made of the Learning Centre,' said Stewart, with a careless laugh. 'I'll bet he'd have turned his nose up at my Creativity Assisted Language Learning System. You've read about CRALLS in the brochure, I expect?' he said proudly, turning back to Melissa. 'Absolute brainwave on my part. Of course, the traditionalists hate it … hate me too, some of them, for being too successful and pinching their customers!' His rather fleshy face, set on a short bull neck, seemed to swell with self-satisfaction, reminding Melissa of a production of *Toad of Toad Hall* that she had seen as a child. Any minute now and he'll go 'Poop-poop!' she thought as she struggled to keep a straight face.

'It sounds most interesting,' she said demurely. 'What form does the creativity part take?'

'Oh, that's Verry's department. She's the arty-crafty one,' he said dismissively. 'More wine?'

'No, thank you,' said Melissa. She looked across the table at Verity and was about to repeat the question, but something in the other woman's expression made her hesitate. Compressed lips and narrowed eyes told of a simmering resentment that might erupt at any moment.

The awkward silence was broken by the warble of the telephone on the dresser. Stewart got up to answer it, spoke a few words and then announced, 'This might go on for a while – I'll take it in the study. You two go ahead and have your dessert.' Apparently oblivious to the tension in the atmosphere, he went out, closing the door behind him.

Verity brought a dish of fruit salad and a jug of cream to the table and sat down, but made no move to serve. Her mouth was set in a hard line and her hands were tightly intertwined.

Melissa waited for a few moments, uncertain what to do or say. At last, Verity took a deep breath and said, in a voice throbbing with barely controlled anger, 'Let me tell you something, Melissa. *I* designed this room, not him. And CRALLS was *my* idea … and this house belongs in *my* family, not his. My little girl … my Tammy … should be growing up here.'

On the final words, her voice cracked; tears spilled from her eyes and her mouth began working. For a few seconds she fought for self control, while Melissa tried desperately to think of some words of comfort. Then she blurted out, 'Help yourself to dessert, I'll be back in a minute,' covered her eyes with a handkerchief and stumbled out of the room.

Feeling utterly helpless, Melissa sat waiting and wishing that she had never accepted Stewart Haughan's invitation. From being merely uncomfortable and embarrassing, the evening had turned into a total disaster.

It was shortly to become a nightmare.

CHAPTER SEVEN

While they ate, the sun had gone down and night closed in unobserved, like a stealthy enemy creeping up on its quarry. The curtains were still open and the darkened windows threw back an image of the brightly lit interior, accurate in every detail yet somehow drained of its intrinsic warmth and comfort and security. Huge moths, drawn to the light, thumped against the glass and settled there, furry wings outspread, antennae quivering, tiny eyes gleaming. Staring at her own reflection, Melissa had a momentary, irrational feeling that it was her actual self out there in unknown territory, exposed to and defenceless against some lurking, indefinable danger.

She thought uneasily of having to cross the yard to the unfamiliar 'cell' where she would be spending the night – and several nights to come – instead of her own bedroom in Hawthorn Cottage. Then she reminded herself that she had experienced similar feelings of disquiet on first moving to the country and told herself not to be a fool. It was no more dangerous here than at home; it was just the strangeness that made her apprehensive.

No ... it was more than that. This was not a happy house, despite the hospitality and the cosiness and the flowers and the chintzy upholstery. There was tension here, a barely contained resentment and anger ... possibly hatred. Such feelings, if allowed to smoulder and feed on themselves, could one day break free with terrible consequences. A sense of foreboding, illogical but overwhelming, made Melissa get to her feet and close the curtains, as if by so doing she could hold the unseen menace at bay.

She returned to her seat at the table and waited. After a few minutes she heard the sound of footsteps overhead, then coming downstairs. The door opened and Stewart Haughan reappeared. 'Sorry about that, ladies,' he said breezily, then frowned. 'Where's Verry?'

'She just popped out for a moment, I don't think she'll be long,' said Melissa, hoping it was true.

He eyed the table. 'You haven't had your dessert.'

'It's all right, we decided to wait for you after all. Ah, here she is.'

The door reopened and Verity entered. She had washed away her tears and tidied her hair, but her face was pale and her smoky eyes were wide with alarm. In her hand, she held a sheet of paper.

'There's another one,' she faltered, holding it out.

Stewart snatched it and read what was written. His face turned turkey-red and his eyes bulged. 'Where did you find it? When did it come?' he shouted at her.

'It was in the hall. Someone must have put it through the letter-box while we were having dinner.'

'Don't lie to me.'

She gave a little gasp and took a step backward as if fearing he was going to strike her. 'I'm not lying,' she protested. 'Why should I lie?'

He took her by the shoulders and thrust his face close to hers. 'Because you wrote it, you cow, that's why! How dare you!' He began shaking her like a rag doll, mouthing obscenities.

Melissa leapt from her chair and grabbed at his arm. 'Stop that! Leave her alone!' she shouted.

It was plain from his shocked expression that he had totally forgotten her presence. Immediately, he let his hands fall to his sides and Verity, trembling but apparently unhurt, went back to her seat at the table.

'Got carried away, didn't I?' he said. He was breathing heavily; whatever was written on the paper had evidently shaken him badly, but he managed a grin that held a touch of bravado as he said, 'Might as well tell Melissa the full story, eh, Verry?' He seemed anxious to make amends, to repair his image in the eyes of his guest. 'Tell you what,' he went on, refilling Melissa's wine-glass without asking and signalling to his wife to serve the neglected dessert, 'maybe you can help us, you being a detective story writer and all that.'

Melissa took the bowl of fruit salad that Verity handed her and helped herself to cream. 'Being a crime writer and being a detective are two very different things,' she pointed out. 'Writers invent their own mysteries and plant their own clues.'

'Granted, but you must have picked up a lot of ideas along the way …'

'Ideas about what? People who send anonymous messages?'

He nodded eagerly. 'You see, you guessed already what the problem is.'

'That wasn't difficult, seeing that I was here when that one arrived.' Melissa wondered how he would react to the knowledge that she had been told of his visit to the police station and had overheard members of his staff discussing the affair. She kept her own counsel on both points. 'How many have you had?' she asked.

'Dunno. Six or seven, maybe.'

She gestured at the paper, still lying where he had slammed it down on the table in his fury. 'May I see that?'

'Of course.' He handed it over. 'If you can make sense of it, you're smarter than I,' – he gave his wife a sidelong glance and corrected himself – 'than we are.'

Melissa unfolded the paper and read the three typewritten lines:

> First, you gave her hope
> Then hope died within her soul
> Will hope die again?

Melissa read it over slowly, aloud, counting off the syllables. 'Did you keep the others?' she asked.

'No, I binned them.' Obviously, he was not going to admit that he had made a fruitless call on the police.

'Can you remember what they said?'

'Not exactly. A lot of rot about winter coming too soon, and blood turning to ice … load of old cobblers really.'

Melissa glanced from one to the other. 'And you've no idea what the writer might be referring to?' she asked.

Verity, her eyes fixed on her untouched plate, said nothing, but Stewart shook his head almost defiantly. 'Haven't a clue,' he said stoutly.

Melissa refolded the paper and handed it back to him. 'I really don't see what I can do to help …' she began, but he cut in eagerly.

'You could ask around a bit … you might pick up something I missed … you'd know the right questions …'

'You mean, you want me to make enquiries among your staff? Won't they think it rather odd for a complete outsider to poke her nose into your affairs?'

'You could make out it's for a story you're writing. Yeah, that's it!' He became fired with enthusiasm. 'I'll tell them you're working on a plot about some crank writing poison pen letters, and I showed you this, just to help you, of course … I mean, I don't want you to run away with the idea that we're seriously worried …' He picked up his glass and leaned nonchalantly back in his chair, once more in control of the situation.

Melissa was tingling with inward excitement. It was almost too good to be true; here he was, giving her carte blanche to do openly what she had been hoping to do surreptitiously. However, she deliberately kept a note of reserve in her voice as she replied, 'Well, if you're sure you don't mind my appearing inquisitive to the people in your office … I can't promise to be much help, but I'll see what I can do …'

'But, aren't you here to be getting on with your own writing? I thought that was the whole idea of a "Writer's Retreat",' Verity interposed.

For a moment, Stewart appeared nonplussed; then his entre-preneurial instincts came to the rescue. 'Sure, sure,' he agreed. 'But I tell you what, Mel, you nail the joker who's been playing silly buggers and I'll give you another week here, absolutely free. Can't say fairer than that, can I?'

'It sounds a reasonable offer,' Melissa agreed with a smile. 'All right, I'll see what I can ferret out.' She glanced at her watch; it was ten o'clock. 'I think, if you'll excuse me, I'll be getting back to my "cell".'

'Make sure the little grey ones get plenty of beauty sleep, eh?' said Stewart jovially. 'Little grey cells … Hercule Poirot,' he added, as if anxious to display his knowledge of classic crime fiction.

'Quite.' Melissa got up from the table. 'Good night, and thank you for a delicious meal,' she said to Verity.

Stewart brought her coat and escorted her to the door. He opened it, switched on the exterior light and stood aside for her to pass him. As she stepped outside, she saw something lying on the ground.

'Oh dear, your lovely hanging basket's fallen down,' she said. She moved forward to inspect the damage and something touched her on the shoulder. She glanced up and gave an involuntary gasp of alarm. Suspended from the bracket that had held the basket was a crude dummy figure, dressed in a woman's clothing. Pinned to the dress was a piece of paper on which was printed, in typewritten capitals, 'THE END OF HOPE IS NIGH'.

CHAPTER EIGHT

'What the hell …?' Stewart gazed up at the effigy, goggle-eyed and open mouthed. The light from the electric lantern above the door showed the colour draining from his face, leaving a naevus of broken veins on either cheek. He put a hand to his mouth and for a moment Melissa thought he was going to throw up. Then he reached out and gingerly grasped the thing by one leg, as if to confirm that it was real and not some grotesque phantasm. One of the shoes fell off; he let go and jumped backwards like a man who has had an electric shock.

'It's sick!' he said hoarsely. 'Plain, bloody sick!'

'What is it?' Verity, hearing the disturbance, appeared in the doorway.

'Another little jest by your husband's unknown correspondent,' said Melissa shakily.

Verity glanced up at the dangling figure and uttered a cry of disgust. 'What does it mean?' she whispered. 'Who would do such a horrible thing?'

'Let's have a look at it. Maybe we can find a clue.' Stewart had pulled himself together and was tugging at the thin rope looped round the bracket. The dummy slumped to the ground and lay propped sideways against the wall with its white straw hat tilted over its face, giving it the appearance of a fallen drunk. Stewart bent over it, then appeared to change his mind. 'Take it indoors, Verry,' he ordered. 'I'm going to have a look round and see what I can find.' He grabbed a flashlight from the hall table and marched off into the darkness.

'I'm not having it in the house,' said Verity in a thin but decided voice. 'We'll take it over to the garage.'

They carried it across the yard; Verity unlocked the garage door and switched on the light. There were two cars inside, but enough space between them to lay the thing on the floor. Together the two women inspected it.

The body was made from a broom handle, thickly padded with newspaper and rammed into a polystyrene head of the type used in stores to display women's hats. A pair of nylon tights, stuffed with more paper, formed the legs; a second pair, pushed through the long sleeves of the flower-sprigged cotton dress and similarly filled, made the arms.

'Now, what does it tell us?' mused Melissa. 'That dress isn't new, but it's in reasonable condition, too good to throw away. I don't suppose you've seen anyone round here wearing it?'

Verity shook her head. 'I don't think so, but I don't go into the office very often.'

'What about one of the students?'

'Not that I remember. No, I'm sure not – I'd have noticed that pattern.'

Melissa peered at the label inside the neck of the dress. 'It's a Laura Ashley design,' she said. 'It might have come from a charity shop.'

Verity gave a shrug. 'There are dozens of those around.'

'Mm. What else can we find out?' Melissa looked at each item in turn. 'The head's the only really distinctive thing. If we enquired around, someone might have seen it – or one like it – on a junk stall. The shoes and hat might have come from the same place as the dress. The tights look brand new.' She straightened up and thought for a moment. 'Now that's interesting, isn't it?'

'Why?'

'If you were going to play a trick like this, you wouldn't use your own old clothes – someone might recognise them – but there'd be no risk in using an old pair of your own tights, would there?'

Verity thought for a moment. 'I suppose not, if you had any. I always wear stockings myself,' she said absently. 'You think it's significant?'

'It seems to point to your husband's anonymous correspondent being a man. Tights are the one thing he wouldn't pick up second-hand, and unless he's a transvestite he wouldn't have any of his own. And he's probably not married, either, or he could pinch a pair his wife had thrown out.'

Verity's tense features seemed to relax a little. 'Oh, I'm glad you think it isn't a woman,' she said earnestly, without looking up. 'Will you tell Stewart? You heard what he said …'

'If you want me to.' Melissa gave her a keen glance, hoping that she might volunteer some further information, but Verity merely continued looking down at the dummy, which had begun to disintegrate under their examination. 'What are we going to do with this?'

'Leave it to Stewart to decide.' Verity dusted her hands and turned on her heel. 'I'm getting cold. Let's go indoors.' She switched off the garage light and gestured to Melissa to move aside while she closed the door.

'I was going back to my room,' Melissa pointed out.

'Oh, please stay with me until Stewart gets back,' Verity begged. 'I don't fancy being on my own. I'll make a cup of tea …' She took Melissa by the arm. 'Please!'

'All right.' They returned to the kitchen and Verity bustled about, filling the kettle and assembling cups and saucers. 'I'm so relieved you think it's not a woman,' she said again. 'I mean, you don't like to think a woman could be so … well … nasty, do you?'

'Oh, some women can be pretty nasty if they feel they have a grievance,' Melissa replied. She walked round the table and stood in front of Verity as she waited by the stove for the water to boil, one hand resting on the handle of the kettle. 'Why did Stewart accuse you of planting that note?' she asked.

Verity gave a nervous half-smile and turned her head away. 'It's nothing really ... just a gut reaction ... he does lose his rag at times ... gets quite unreasonable ... speaks without thinking ... it doesn't last ...' The words trailed unconvincingly away, but before Melissa had time to question her further, there was the sound of footsteps outside. The outer door crashed open and then slammed shut; Stewart entered, dumped the flashlight on the dresser and began marching up and down the room, his hands in his pockets and his face set and angry. He seemed short of breath, as if he had been running.

'Whoever it was must have got in over the back wall. There are footprints across the potato patch where Martin's been digging,' he said. 'I'll have a closer look tomorrow, in daylight.' He stopped pacing and looked at Melissa. 'Did you figure anything out?'

'She's pretty sure it's a man doing all this,' Verity interposed before Melissa had time to answer.

'Well, of course it is. There's quite a clever brain at work here,' said Stewart.

'I had the impression that you suspected Verity,' said Melissa icily.

Mindless of the fact that he had said something deeply offensive to his wife and guest, Stewart switched on a disarming smile that made him suddenly and devastatingly attractive. '*Moi*? It never entered my head,' he said in a voice of honey, and before either of the women had a chance to challenge the blatant lie, he went on, 'I reckon it's one of my competitors trying to wind me up, put me off my stroke and upset my employees. Said as much the other day, didn't I, Verry?' The smile vanished as suddenly as it had appeared and he banged a closed fist on the table. 'These bloody stupid messages – and tonight's bit of crap – are just a warm-up. I've got to nail the bugger before he does something to upset my clients and get my business a bad name.' He turned to Melissa. 'Just get on with it, Mel. The police don't want to know, sod them.'

Melissa was about to retort that she was a paying client herself, not an employee to be given orders, but she changed her mind and let it pass. With luck, there would be other opportunities to put him in his place; for the moment, her objective was to extract more information.

'You didn't tell me you'd been to the police,' she said. It would be interesting to hear his version of the interview. 'What did they say?'

'Some pompous underling gave me a load of bullshit about it not being a police matter unless I could show that I was being threatened. I consider I *am* being threatened if I'm targeted by some half-wit who should be locked away. I'm running a legitimate business here, I pay my taxes and those useless w – – – – – s say they can't do a bloody thing about it. Too busy harassing motorists to protect law-abiding citizens.'

Melissa had no intention of becoming involved in an argument over police responsibility. She tried another approach. 'How have the previous messages been delivered?' she asked.

'Some by post, some I found among my papers.'

'In your private office?'

'Right – at least, that's where they've mostly come to light. They've probably been put there in the general office.'

'Who has access to that, apart from the people who work there?'

'Pretty well everyone, it's very free and easy here. Teachers go in and out to make photocopies, students call in to borrow books and tapes …'

'They just walk in and help themselves?'

'If George Ballard isn't there – he's only part-time – they go to his cupboard, take what they want and enter it in the book.'

'So there are plenty of opportunities for someone to slip a message among your papers unobserved?'

'I suppose so.'

'And you're quite sure none of your employees is involved?'

Stewart let out an unexpected guffaw. 'I reckon to keep them too busy to waste time on crappy poems,' he declared. 'I've questioned them all, of course – they claim to know nothing about it. No reason why any of them should bear a grudge – they know that if they've got a moan, they can come to me in person. I'm always ready to listen to a genuine complaint.' His air of sweet reasonableness would have convinced the most sceptical.

Remembering a comment by Ken Harris, Melissa said, 'So you've no idea at all what these poems are referring to?'

'Not the faintest.'

"Hope' is sometimes used as a girl's name. You don't happen to know a girl or a woman called that?'

'No.'

'Not among your employees?' He shook his head emphatically. 'What about students – do you know them by the first names?'

'Usually – but we haven't had any Hopes.' He made a gesture of impatience. 'Look, I told you what I think's behind this.'

'You mean, you believe someone wants to damage your business? It seems an odd way to go about it, but … if no member of the staff is involved, could it be someone masquerading as a student?'

'I suppose it could … but there haven't been any students here today.'

'That might explain why this person chose a different means of making this evening's delivery.'

His face lit up and he clapped his hands. 'Mel, I do believe you're on to something. Let's think this through now.' He planted his elbows on the table and leaned towards her. His expression was eager; he was obviously prepared to carry on with the discussion indefinitely, but Melissa decided she had done enough for one evening.

'Look,' she said, a little wearily, 'it's getting late and I'm really rather tired. I suggest that tomorrow you check the people who were enrolled on courses on the days when you received the other messages … find out if any of them gave false information about who they work for, that sort of thing.' She drank the lukewarm tea that Verity had poured some minutes ago and got to her feet. 'Now, if you'll excuse me, I really must get some sleep. There's no need to see me out,' she added firmly and made for the door, leaving Stewart with the wind temporarily taken out of his sails.

Before getting ready for bed, she made some notes about the day's events, reflecting wryly that, had she not made a quick getaway, Stewart would probably have kept her up for half the night, raising more points, asking more questions and ending up accepting her suggestions and dumping responsibility for following them up in her own lap. He had come across as a wholly self-centred character who would say and do whatever seemed expedient at the moment, regardless of truth or the feelings or rights of others. Despite the apparently innocuous nature of the messages, she was becoming convinced that something sinister lay behind them. Someone, somewhere, was nursing a bitter animosity towards Stewart Haughan. To what lengths was that person prepared to go?

There were other questions to be answered. What reason did Stewart have for accusing his wife of sending the messages – an accusation which he had subsequently denied? And how – if at all – did the former employee, whose name was not Hope but Kate and who had since died, fit into the picture?

CHAPTER NINE

Melissa slept fitfully in the unfamiliar surroundings and awoke soon after five. She showered, dressed in a sweatshirt and jeans, made a cup of tea and sat down at the desk where, on arrival, she had left the draft of her current novel. That, she reminded herself, was ostensibly why she was here, although curiosity about the source and purpose of the haiku messages had also played a part. And for the moment, it was those strange little poems, with their melancholy themes, that occupied her mind and made it impossible to concentrate on her writing.

She had memorised the text of the previous evening's poem and jotted it down as soon as she was on her own. She took out her copies of the two that Ken Harris had shown her, laid all three on the desk and sat for a long time studying them:

> Spring ended too soon
> With no summer to follow
> Winter is so cold
> Her blood became ice
> She sleeps in winter's embrace
> Never to awake
> First, you gave her hope
> Then hope died within her soul
> Will hope die again?

Some while ago, Iris had shown her a book on haiku. She remembered idly skimming through it, wondering – as she did with most odd scraps of knowledge that came her way – whether it contained anything that might come in handy for use in a mystery novel. Having reached the conclusion that it did not, she had returned it, hardly giving the subject another thought until now.

'A moment of beauty, wonder, or sadness', was the phrase that had stuck in her mind. There was sadness here, no doubt about that. There had also been a reference to the seasons, as there was in two of these poems … but not in the latest. Was that significant? There had been earlier ones, which Haughan claimed had been destroyed … they might have held further clues …

'Damn!' said Melissa, impatiently sweeping up the scraps of paper and shoving them back into her folder. 'How did I get myself involved in this nonsense? If I'd never read that stupid book … where did Iris get hold of it anyway? Oh yes, some man she'd met whose hobby was poetry. Maybe he could shed some light on the puzzle. It wouldn't hurt to have a word with him, if Iris was still in touch.'

Melissa checked the time; it was still only a little after six, much too early to call Iris. In any case, there was no phone in her room; she would have to wait until the office opened. Meanwhile, she would go for a walk before breakfast.

It was a perfect September morning of cool, clean air and dew-spangled cobwebs. The eastern sky was a sheet of flame where the rising sun lit up the underside of a patch of broken cloud. Vapour trails left by aircraft heading for London became glittering golden threads where they were touched by the light. It was harvest time and a huge combine, parked in one corner of a half-cut field of ripe grain, waited to tackle another day's work.

To the west, beyond a small orchard, the land dropped away to form a shallow valley carpeted with white swirls of mist. From a branch laden with rosy fruit, a blackbird uttered an insistent warning call as a cat picked its stealthy way through the grass.

A path led through the trees, away from the house, and Melissa followed it until something white caught her eye. It was a small caravan, doubtless the one occupied by Martin Morris. She decided to turn back, rather than invade his private domain.

Then she saw the man himself, a short distance to her right. He had his back towards her and was bending down as if looking at something on the ground, but whatever had caught his attention was hidden from her view. After a moment, he straightened up, took a step backwards and remained for several seconds as if transfixed. Then, like someone simulating slow motion, he raised cupped hands to his face and covered his eyes:

In half a dozen paces, Melissa was at his side, staring in alarm into the shallow ditch where a man, his head half covered by the hood of a cotton sweatshirt, lay face down and motionless.

'Who is it?' she whispered. 'Is he dead?'

Martin appeared paralysed with shock. 'How does one tell?' he asked dazedly.

Melissa knelt in the damp grass and reached for one wrist. There was still some warmth there, but she could feel no pulse. She took the head, gently lifted it and turned the man's face clear of the dried mud and grass at the bottom of the ditch.

'My God!' she exclaimed. 'It's Stewart Haughan!'

His eyes were closed and his face had a bluish tinge, except for two pale patches on his nose and forehead where they had been in contact with the ground. Melissa had seen pictures of post-mortem lividity; what she saw now looked horribly like the real thing.

She stood up. Her head swam a little from stooping and she clutched at Martin for support. 'I think he's dead,' she muttered, 'or if not, he's in a bad way. We must call a doctor at once. And Verity will have to be told. Shall I go, or will you?'

Martin was still gazing at the body as if in a dream. 'Are you sure there's nothing we can do for him?' he said.

'Better not touch him.' His indecision in a crisis was beginning to irritate her. 'You wait here; I'll be as quick as I can.' She turned and sped back to the house without giving him time to argue.

The couple of minutes spent jabbing the bellpush seemed like an hour. At last she heard shuffling footsteps along the passage.

'Who's there?' called Verity.

'It's Melissa. Let me in, quickly.'

Verity had thrown on a blue candlewick dressing gown without bothering to fasten it and she clutched it round her slight body with one hand as she held the door open with the other. From her tousled hair, flushed face and puffy eyes, it was clear that she had been awakened from a deep sleep. 'What is it?' she asked in a husky voice.

'It's Stewart. We found him lying in the orchard. I'm afraid he's … we must phone for a doctor.'

Verity's eyes widened and her mouth opened and closed as if she had difficulty in drawing breath. Then she said, almost in a whisper, 'Has he had an accident?'

'We don't know what happened. He's just lying there, not moving. Martin found him … please, Verity, call the doctor right away.'

'You'd better do it. You'll know what to tell him.' Verity turned and led the way into the kitchen, handed Melissa the phone and indicated a number scribbled on a memo board. Shock had drained the colour from her face and she wore a dazed expression.

Melissa punched out the number; a Doctor Brizewell answered and, to her relief, promised to attend immediately without asking too many detailed questions. When she put the phone down, Verity's eyes had lost their glassy look and become focused.

'He's dead, isn't he?' she said in a flat, tired voice.

'I don't know for certain, but it does look like it,' Melissa replied gently. 'Martin is with him. I'll stay here until the doctor comes. Would you like me to make some tea or coffee?'

'No ... no thank you. I must have a wash and tidy up before Doctor Brizewell gets here.' Verity put a hand to her hair and then pulled the dressing gown more closely round her, shivering slightly. 'I'll be all right ... I'd rather be on my own, really ... you go back and tell Martin the doctor's on his way.'

'You're in shock ... I don't think I should leave you by yourself.'

'I want to be alone. Please.'

'If you're sure.'

'I'm sure.'

Martin was still standing in exactly the same spot, in exactly the same attitude, as when Melissa had left him.

'The doctor said he'd be here in ten minutes,' she said.

He nodded without looking at her. 'What do you think happened?' he asked.

'I've no idea, but I'd say he was unconscious when he fell.'

'What makes you say that?'

'From the position of his arms, it doesn't look as if he made any attempt to break his fall. He might have had a heart attack, or some kind of fit, I suppose.' A thought struck her and she continued, half to herself, 'I wonder if he was out looking for traces of the person who left that poem here last evening. He said he'd come and search when it was light.'

For the first time, Martin took his eyes from the still form and looked at her. There was bewilderment in his expression. 'Someone left a poem last evening? Like the ones he's been getting in the office?'

'The same sort of thing. It was pushed through his letter-box. When I left – I'd been invited for dinner – we found an effigy of a woman hanging outside his door. He went rushing off to see if he could catch whoever had done it, but of course they'd long gone.'

Martin put a hand to his forehead. 'There's something very strange here,' he muttered. 'What did the poem say?'

'Something about hope dying in someone's soul ... and there was another message pinned to the dummy figure ... not a poem this time, but still on about the end of hope.'

'Very strange,' he repeated. 'I don't understand ... it doesn't make sense.' He seemed to be thinking aloud rather than speaking to her, as if trying to interpret what had happened in relation to something else. She was instantly curious.

'What do you mean?' she asked, but before he could reply, the sound of a car driven at speed up the drive made them both turn round.

'That'll be the doctor,' said Martin. She had the impression that he was relieved at not having to reply to her question. 'I'll go and meet him.'

Doctor Brizewell was middle-aged and tired-looking, having been – as he was at pains to inform them – a mere half-hour from going off duty when Melissa's call came through. He plodded wearily across to where Stewart was lying, put his case on the ground and squatted down to begin his examination.

'Has he been moved?' he asked.

'His face was hidden, so I turned his head in case his nose and mouth were blocked,' Melissa replied. 'We were afraid to do anything else – that's why we called you straight away.'

The doctor nodded and drew aside the hood of Stewart's sweatshirt, which still partially covered the back of his head and neck. He ran a finger along the base of the skull and then spent several seconds examining the hood itself. Then he stood up and brushed grass seeds from his trousers.

'He's dead all right,' he said. 'I can't give the cause of death without a post-mortem, but the police must be informed. Will one of you go back to the house and call them?'

'Why the police?' asked Martin. His voice sounded unsteady and Melissa noticed that a pasty tinge had replaced his normally ruddy colour.

'It's usual in the circumstances.' Doctor Brizewell was giving nothing away, but Melissa had spotted the yellowish grains on the cotton hood and guessed that he had come to the same conclusion as herself. She was about to offer to make the call when Martin swung round in a jerky movement, like a puppet responding to a tug on its string.

'I'll call them,' he said. As he hurried away, the combine harvester clattered into harsh, metallic life.

CHAPTER TEN

A police car raced up the drive and stopped by the main entrance to the house. Two uniformed officers got out and were greeted by Doctor Brizewell, who led them along the path to where the body lay.

Had Melissa been on her own before they arrived, she would have been tempted to poke around to see if Stewart's attacker – she was convinced that he had been attacked, almost certainly from behind – had left any clues, but with the doctor present it had been out of the question. As it was, watching him pointing and gesticulating but unable to catch a word of what he was saying, she felt frustrated and superfluous.

She had been up since five o'clock, it was now half-past seven and she had nothing inside her but one cup of tea. The thought of food was uninviting, but she was beginning to feel cold and would have sold her soul for a cup of coffee.

She crossed her arms and hugged her shoulders, shivering and wondering if she could slip away unnoticed. If they wanted to question her, they could find her easily enough.

Some conclusion seemed to have been reached. One of the officers left the group and headed back to the police car; the other turned and approached Melissa.

'Good morning, Madam, I'm Sergeant Powell. I understand that you found the body,' he said courteously.

'No, actually it was the gardener, Martin Morris. I was out for a walk, I saw him standing there and I could tell something was wrong, so I came over.'

'And what did you do then?'

'I felt for a pulse and couldn't find one. Then I moved the face clear of the earth and I thought he looked pretty bad, so I ran back to the house, alerted Mrs Haughan and called the doctor.'

'And your name is …?' Melissa gave it, half expecting some sign of recognition, but there was none. 'Are you a member of the family or a guest here?'

'A paying guest, actually. Uphanger accommodates writers who want a few days' peace and quiet to work on their books.'

'You're a writer, Madam?'

'Yes.' Again, the reaction was neutral. Melissa felt a momentary disappointment, followed by a sense of shame. A man lay dead, in all probability murdered, and she had the cheek to feel miffed because one police officer failed to recognise her name.

'I understand it was a Mr Morris who made the 999 call,' Powell continued. 'That would be the gardener, I take it? Do you happen to know where he is now?'

'I think he must be still in the house. He lives over there,' she nodded in the direction of the caravan, 'but I haven't seen him come back.'

'And Mr Haughan's wife … widow?'

'I presume she's in the house as well. That's where I left her.'

'Thank you, Madam.' He shut his notebook and put it in his pocket. 'My colleague has radioed headquarters and a senior detective will be along shortly, together with Scene of Crime Officers … and an ambulance. Meanwhile, perhaps you will be kind enough to return to the house and wait there with the others for the time being.'

'Yes, of course.'

'Is there anyone else on the premises?'

Melissa glanced at her watch. 'Not yet, so far as I know. The office staff will be arriving some time after eight o'clock, I imagine. I can't tell you much about them – I only arrived here yesterday – but the reception desk is off the hall, just inside the main door. That's where you'll find them.'

He thanked her again and rejoined his colleague, while Melissa went to find Verity and put her in the picture. Finding the courtyard door ajar, she went in and made her way along the passage to the kitchen. That door was not completely closed either; Martin must have left both unlatched in his haste to reach the telephone. Melissa raised her hand to knock, then froze as she heard Martin say, in a low, urgent voice, 'I know it looks bad, but I didn't kill him, I swear it.'

'They're just as likely to suspect me.' Now it was Verity speaking. 'They'll say I had a motive.'

'They won't know about that if you keep quiet.'

'They'll find out. They might even suspect the pair of us ... think it's some sort of conspiracy. Oh my God, what are we going to do?'

There was a silence, during which Melissa had a furious tussle with her conscience. It was evident that the relationship between Verity and Martin was closer than that of employer and employee, but that did not necessarily mean they were having an affair. What she had witnessed the previous evening had revealed deep divisions between husband and wife, but the world, sadly, was full of unhappy marriages of which only a fraction led to murder. Besides, she had a strong feeling that Haughan had been felled with a blow to the head, and found it difficult to imagine a slightly built woman like Verity being capable of the necessary force.

Martin was a horse of a different colour. Despite his air of shock on finding the body, his surprise at hearing of last night's events and the protestation of innocence she had just overheard – all of which seemed absolutely genuine – it was clear that he and Verity each had something to hide. If she continued to listen she might hear more. On the other hand, the door might open at any moment and reveal her presence to those inside. If either of them *was* the killer, it might not be very clever to let them know that their incriminating remarks had been overheard. Discretion seemed to be the name of the game. She tiptoed back to the front door, stepped outside and rang the bell.

Peggy Drage leaned her elbows on her desk, propped her face in her hands and for the umpteenth time muttered, 'I can't believe it.' Every so often she dabbed at her eyes with a tissue and sniffed.

George Ballard, wrestling with the yards of plastic tape that secured a newly delivered parcel of books, gave her a sharp look. 'You don't have to pretend to be upset,' he said.

'I'm not pretending. It's a dreadful thing to have happened.'

'I wouldn't let anyone see you crying over him if I were you. They might get the wrong idea.'

'That's a horrible thing to say!' It was not the first time that she had been shocked by his cynicism. 'A man's dead and you don't seem to care in the slightest.'

'Oh, I care all right. The chances are that I'll lose my job. We'll all lose our jobs.'

'Not necessarily. Mrs Haughan may carry on with the Centre. I'm sure she'll want to go on living at Uphanger – the house belongs to her.'

George stopped in the act of checking the contents of the parcel. 'It does? How do you know that?'

'She inherited it from a relative. There was something about it in a letter from a solicitor. I wasn't supposed to see it … Stewart passed it to me by mistake and then grabbed it back.'

He gave a soft whistle. 'You never said.'

'I was his secretary, wasn't I? That sort of thing's confidential.'

'And now the business will be hers as well. Very nice too.'

Peggy rounded on him. 'How can you talk like that when her husband's just been brutally murdered?' She gulped and dabbed again at her reddened eyes.

'If he treated her the way he treated you … treated all of us … she's probably glad to see the back of him.'

Peggy looked at him in disgust. 'You … you're unbelievable! I've never heard anything so callous.'

'Don't be so mealy-mouthed. Everyone knows he was a prize bastard.'

'Not all the time. He could be very charming.' The tears began to flow again.

'Oh yes, we know all about that, don't we?'

'Don't …' Peggy broke off at the sound of footsteps crossing the hall. Pam appeared with a tray of coffee and set it on the counter.

'I wonder if that policeman waiting outside would like some,' she said. 'I'll go and ask him.' She went to the front door just as Sadie came bursting in.

'Whatever's going on?' she demanded, her eyes wide and her smooth young cheeks bright pink. 'That policeman outside wouldn't tell me anything, but there's lots of people crawling about in the orchard … and police cars everywhere …'

'Stewart's been topped,' said George. He took out the last of the books, threw the empty box under the counter and picked up a mug of coffee. Sadie clapped a hand to her mouth and burst into tears.

Pam put an arm round her and frowned at George. 'You might put things a bit more gently,' she reproached him, stroking Sadie's hair and patting her on the shoulder. 'We don't know exactly what happened. All we've been told is that he was found dead in the orchard. He might have had a heart attack.'

George gave a superior, knowing smirk. 'The fuzz don't turn out in force for someone who's keeled over from natural causes.'

Sadie dried her eyes, ducked under the counter and went over to her desk. 'I suppose we'll all have to answer questions,' she speculated. The thought seemed to cheer her up. 'It'll be just like something on the telly.'

Peggy put away her handkerchief and got up to fetch the pile of unopened letters that the postman had left on the counter. 'I don't think we should just sit around discussing it,' she said. 'And it's hardly entertainment,' she added, with a glance of reproof at Sadie.

'Oh, I know ... but it is exciting, isn't it? Like a Mel Craig murder mystery.' Sadie's grief and shock were fading as suddenly as they had appeared. 'I wonder if she'll be helping the police with their enquiries.'

'Not unless she's a suspect,' said George drily. The thought seemed to afford him considerable amusement. 'That's police and newspaper jargon for being detained for questioning,' he explained, as Sadie looked blank.

Peggy gave a sudden exclamation of alarm and fished a file from a drawer in her desk. 'I've just remembered, our other writer in retreat is arriving this morning,' she said agitatedly. 'Do you think I ought to tell him not to come?'

'He's probably left home already,' said Pam.

'He might not, he's only coming from Stowbridge. It's worth a try.' Peggy reached for the telephone, but at that moment they heard the front door open and close. Everyone looked round as a tall, grey-haired man in a raincoat, a canvas holdall in one hand, approached the counter.

'Ben Strickland,' he announced. 'Remember me? I've been looking forward to this return visit, but it seems I've arrived at an awkward moment.'

CHAPTER ELEVEN

Martin came in response to Melissa's ring. He looked anxious; when he saw who was there, his relief was visible.

'I thought you were the police,' he said, standing aside for her to enter.

'They'll be along presently.' She paused in front of the kitchen door. 'Is Verity in here?'

As if for the moment he had taken charge, he said, 'Yes, go right in.'

Verity was sitting at the table, clasping a mug of coffee so tightly that the bones in her small hands stood out as if the flesh had been shrink-wrapped round them. She stared at the wall, her eyes blank, moving her lips like an actor silently repeating a part. Martin, one hand half extended, made a move towards her, then changed direction, went over to the window and stood there with his back to it, watching.

'If there's any more of that coffee, I'd appreciate a cup,' said Melissa.

The words roused Verity out of her lethargy. With a jerky movement she put down her own mug and stumbled to her feet, immediately the apologetic hostess.

'How awful of me … you haven't had any breakfast or anything … shall I make you some toast?'

'Maybe later. Coffee will be fine for now.'

Verity served Melissa with coffee and mimed with the cafetière an offer to refill Martin's mug, but he shook his head. Melissa helped herself to milk from a carton on the table and swallowed several mouthfuls before saying carefully, 'They don't know yet how Stewart died, but there will be detectives here soon to make a routine examination of the scene. They'll want to talk to us, so we're to wait here until they arrive.'

'The doctor must think it's suspicious or he wouldn't have called for the police,' said Verity in a small, thin voice.

'Any sudden, unexplained death is treated as suspicious. There'll be a post-mortem to establish the cause.'

'We can guess that. Somebody slugged him didn't they?' said Martin.

'There's no point in speculating,' said Melissa guardedly. She looked from one to the other. 'Tell me,' she went on, speaking slowly, thinking on her feet, 'with hindsight, can you remember if any of the haiku poems that Stewart received, apart from last night's, contained anything at all that could be construed as a threat?'

Martin gave her a sharp look and before Verity could speak, he asked, 'What did you call them?'

'The poem I saw' – remembering that she had officially seen only one, she was careful not to say 'poems' – 'was in a Japanese verse form called haiku. I had the impression that they were all in a similar form ... I may be wrong, of course. It may not have any particular significance,' she went on. 'I don't know enough about it.' But I intend to find out more, she promised herself.

'I didn't see anything threatening about the ones Stewart showed me, not in the way you mean,' Verity said unsteadily. 'They were just ... very sad.'

Her voice all but disappeared on the final word.

A new thought struck Melissa. 'Has Stewart ever had dealings with a Japanese company that went sour? Or any Japanese students ... one who might have some kind of grievance, for example?'

Slowly, with puckered brow, Verity shook her head. 'We have had several Japanese students, but Stewart never mentioned any problems. As you know, he had a theory that a competitor might be waging some kind of psychological warfare against him. That's why he went to the police, but they didn't see it his way.'

'They'll be having second thoughts about that now,' said Martin grimly.

Melissa nodded. Another question was burning to be asked, but she could not bring herself to probe an open wound in front of a third party, even one who, according to what she had overheard, might already know the answer. She finished her coffee and was suddenly aware of feeling empty. 'I think I'd like that toast now, if it isn't too much trouble,' she said.

'Of course.' Verity put slices of bread into a toaster and fetched butter and marmalade. 'What about you, Martin?'

'Yes, please … and you ought to try and eat something as well,' he replied. Their eyes met in a glance so brief that Melissa could not have said with certainty that it held any significance.

The three of them ate in silence and had almost finished when the telephone rang. It was Peggy, calling from the office, to say that the second 'writer in retreat' had arrived and been shown to his room, and also that a Detective Chief Inspector Harris would be along shortly to ask a few questions.

'What the hell are you doing here?' demanded Harris in a low voice.

Melissa, facing him across the table in the small dining-room where, had things been different, she would have taken a leisurely breakfast before settling down to write, pretended to look shocked.

'Is that how you normally tackle a witness? No wonder people complain about police intimidation.'

'I tried to call you last night and all I got was your answering machine. Why didn't you say you were coming here? How long are you staying?'

'I suppose anything I say will be taken down and may be used as evidence,' mocked Melissa. 'Ken, I don't have to account for my movements to you or anyone else.'

'I was worried about you. That cottage is so isolated.'

'I have Iris next door.'

'I know … I called her. She pretended not to know where you were, but I could tell she was covering up.'

'You've got a nerve. Anyone would think I was a suspect.'

'Technically, I suppose you are at the moment.' He grinned and she became aware – as always – of the charm of the man, despite the homely features and the tendency to fleshiness. Her irritation evaporated and she smiled back as she replied, 'Then we'd better get on with the interview, hadn't we?'

'Right. Let's begin with this morning.' In response to his questions, she described how she had come upon Martin Morris in the orchard, standing over what had turned out to be Stewart's body. He made notes, from time to time referring back to previous pages and nodding. When she had answered all his questions, he said, 'Okay, that confirms what those two in there,' – he jerked his pen over his shoulder – 'have told me. Now, let's go back to last night. I gather you spent yesterday evening with the Haughans. How did that come about?'

'Haughan explained that "writers in retreat" normally have their meals in this room; a woman comes in from the village to do the cooking. As there was no one but me here last night, they invited me to have dinner with them. We ate in the kitchen.'

'So what happened?'

'I got here about seven thirty. We'd had our first course when there was a phone call. Stewart went to another room to take it. While he was out, Verity got upset over things he'd been saying earlier.' Melissa recounted everything as accurately as she could. 'She left the room in tears. When she came back, she was holding another message which she'd found in the hall by the front door.'

'Did she come back before or after Haughan had finished on the phone?'

Melissa thought for a moment. 'He got back a moment or two before she did.' As soon as she had spoken, she saw what Harris was leading up to.

'Would he have had to cross the hall?'

'I imagine so.'

'But he never saw the message lying there?'

'Obviously not.'

'And no one heard or saw it being delivered?'

'No, but … Ken, I can't believe Verity only pretended to find it. Her shock and surprise were genuine – I could swear to it.'

'And how did Haughan react?'

'Very violently. He came out with a wild accusation that she'd written it herself. Then he started on about business competitors conducting psychological warfare. To be honest, I think he was a bit unbalanced … even in the short time I knew him, he had some very marked swings of mood.'

'Any idea why it should occur to him that his wife had written the poems?'

'Because they hint at the death of a very young female. While he was out of the room, Verity referred to "my Tammy" and said she should have been growing up here, which suggests that they lost a little girl.'

Harris nodded. 'That's a possible explanation.'

'Which she strenuously denies.'

'She would, wouldn't she? So what happened next?'

Melissa went on to give a brief account of the rest of the evening, culminating in the discovery of the effigy hanging outside the front door. When Harris had finished making notes, she asked, 'Has Verity – Mrs Haughan – any idea why her husband was out so early?'

'She claims not to have been aware of him getting up to go out. She thinks he must have decided to look for traces of last night's intruder. Morris says he found him soon after six and Doctor Brizewell examined him about half an hour later. He wouldn't be pinned down, but he thought Haughan had been dead maybe a couple of hours.'

'So we're talking about some time before five o'clock,' said Melissa. 'Why would he go out before the sun was up?'

'It gets light well before sunrise, especially on a clear morning like today.'

'Even so, you'd think he'd have waited … unless he heard someone in the garden. Or maybe the killer lured him outside by ringing the doorbell … but then, Verity would have heard it as well.'

'She says she took a sleeping pill and never heard a thing.'

'That figures. It took me ages to rouse her, after we found Stewart.'

Harris sat for a minute or two, apparently deep in thought, before saying in a brisker tone, 'Now to the office staff. I've had a brief word with them, but it seems none of them was here before about eight-fifteen. Can you tell me anything about them?'

'Not a lot. I overheard one or two remarks when I arrived that made me think the deceased wasn't universally popular and that he didn't exactly overpay them. There's a man there – I understand he's a part-timer in charge of book loans and things like that – who seems to think the women in particular were … undervalued, I think is the best word to describe it.' She repeated George's remarks as accurately as she could remember them.

'From what I'm hearing about Haughan as an employer, I'm surprised any of them stayed,' Harris remarked.

'I don't suppose they had much choice. They're probably thankful to have a job at all nowadays.'

He grunted. 'You're probably right. And if he was unpopular with his employees, he probably had enemies outside as well. That's not going to make our job any easier. Well, I think that's all for now until we have the result of the post-mortem.'

'He was killed by a blow to the head, wasn't he?'

'It looks like it.'

'Ken, do you think those poems were sent by the killer?'

'Officially, I have an open mind. Between ourselves, I'd say it's a strong possibility. I'm turning them over to forensics to see what they make of them.' He closed his notebook and stood up as if to go, then sat down again. 'One other thing. What's your impression of Morris – the gardener?'

'Martin? He seems pleasant enough, well-educated, not the sort of person you'd expect to find doing that job, but maybe he can't find work in his own profession – if he has one.'

'That's what he told me. He's a qualified architect.'

'Oh well, that explains it.' Melissa gave a slightly contemptuous laugh. 'Maybe that's why Haughan employed him, rather than a qualified gardener – he wouldn't have to pay him so much.'

The next question was one she had hoped to avoid. 'Would you say there was anything between him and Mrs Haughan?'

Throughout the interview, the exchanges she had overheard in the kitchen had been in the back of her mind. On the rational level, she knew that it was her duty as a citizen to repeat them, but she honestly believed that Martin had been telling the truth when he swore to Verity that he was not Stewart's killer. And despite Harris's obvious suspicions, nothing would persuade her that Verity, no matter how bitter her feelings towards her husband, was capable of such a deed. Aware that she was hesitating and that the detective's laser-keen eyes were searching hers, she said slowly, 'He did give the impression, when I came back here to deliver Sergeant Powell's message, that he had … sort of taken charge. His manner towards Verity seemed solicitous … a little protective even … but perfectly correct.' Recovering her poise, she met Harris's gaze steadily. 'It was just an impression, that's all I can say.'

'You saw no open intimacy between them?'

'Oh no, nothing like that.' That was true; she had *seen* nothing compromising.

'Well, I'd best be going.' He put away his notebook, stood up again and made for the door. 'How long are you planning to stay here?'

'Until Friday. I'm finishing a book and I only came to get away from the telephone … and possessive policemen.'

He gave another grin. 'Okay, I get the message. Let me know if you pick up anything that might be useful, won't you?'

'Don't tell me you're asking for my help in your investigations,' she said mischievously.

'You know what I'm talking about. You're here on the spot – it's just possible you might learn something useful.'

'I shall be your eyes and ears,' she promised him.

It was a commitment that was to lead her into some deep and dangerous waters.

CHAPTER TWELVE

With her head a jumble of conflicting ideas, Melissa left the house and crossed the courtyard to what Stewart had grandiosely referred to as the 'guest wing'. A stiff breeze had sprung up with a chilly edge to it, a reminder that summer was over. Despite wearing a thick sweatshirt, she shivered as she fumbled in her pocket for her key. Before she had time to put it in her lock, a nearby door opened and a man came out.

'Mel Craig, the crime writer, I believe,' he said.

She turned to look at him and liked what she saw. 'That's right,' she said with a friendly smile. 'You must be another "writer in retreat".'

'Ben Strickland. Delighted to meet you.'

She held out a hand and he gave it a brisk shake. He had deep-set brown eyes, strong, regular features and a firm chin. She judged him to be about sixty. 'Ben Strickland,' she repeated 'I know that name … you write for the *Gazette*, don't you? Consumer reports, special investigations, that sort of thing.'

'The same.' He bobbed his head in acknowledgment, evidently pleased to be so recognised. 'I gather there's been some excitement. The place is swarming with fuzz and the office staff seem to be at sixes and sevens … all I could get out of the woman who brought me over here was, "there's been an accident".'

'No accident. Someone killed Stewart Haughan in the orchard. He's dead.'

'Good God! When?'

'Early this morning.'

Ben ran nicotine-stained fingers through his grizzled hair. 'Who'd have believed it?' he muttered, half to himself. 'Knew he wasn't flavour of the month with quite a few people, but … are you sure he's dead?'

'Oh yes. I was the second person on the scene, and I was there when the doctor examined him.'

'You were?' Ben's air of shocked bewilderment swiftly gave way to the inquisitorial manner of the professional journalist. 'Come in, have a coffee and tell me all.' She hesitated, but he took her by the arm and practically propelled her through his own door.

The room was a replica of her own, except that it appeared to have been struck by a minor earthquake. Books, papers, clothes and toilet articles were scattered over every available surface. Ben scooped up the raincoat, anorak and tweed hat that had been dumped on the armchair and threw them on the floor. 'Sit down,' he said. 'The kettle has boiled … I was just about to have mine when I spotted you going past.' He spooned out granules and poured hot water.

'I've already had coffee, thanks …' she began.

'Not this kind, I'll bet!' He brandished a silver hip flask that he took from his pocket, tipped a capful of its contents into each steaming mug and handed one to Melissa. 'Caribbean rum … the real McCoy … only way to make this instant muck drinkable.' He pulled the chair out from under the desk, lifted a stack of bulging files from the seat, slapped them on top of an already precarious-looking heap and sat down. 'Quite well equipped, these cabins,' he observed with a glance round. 'Good working environment.' He grinned and the furrows running from nose to chin made triangular brackets on either side of his mouth. Seeing Melissa's eyes taking in the disorder, he gestured with his mug and said, 'Can't work if things are too tidy … makes me feel regimented. One of the reasons why I was glad to get out of the army.'

Melissa sipped her coffee with a sigh of appreciation. 'Mm, that's good.' She passed a hand across her eyes and combed her hair back from her face with her fingers. 'I feel as if I've done a day's work already, and I haven't written a line.'

'Never mind, you'll catch up. Fill me in on what's happened here. I see they've put Deadpan Harris on the case.'

Melissa felt her eyebrows lift in surprise. Then came the thought that 'Deadpan' wasn't an inappropriate nickname for a man who rarely smiled, although when he did ... she hastily abandoned that line of thought and did her best to convey detached amusement as she said, 'Is that what he's known as?'

Ben's eyes twinkled above the flame of the match he was using to light a cigarette. 'Among other things. Suits him, doesn't it?'

Melissa shrugged. 'I suppose so. Tell me, what prompted that remark about Stewart not being "flavour of the month". Did you know him?'

'I ran a creative writing course for him during the summer. He practically fawned on the students, was just about civil to the teachers and treated his staff – and his wife – like servants. *And* I had to wait over a month for my money. Not a nice man.'

'That's been my impression, and I only met him yesterday.'

'And now he's been topped. Was it premeditated, do you think?'

'Almost certainly. There's a scoop for you ... I doubt if it'll be included in today's press briefing.'

Ben thought for a moment, then shook his head. 'It's tempting, but I'm supposed to be on a sabbatical. Writing my memoirs,' he explained.

'That's a pity,' said Melissa impulsively. A wild notion had come into her head and set her nerve ends twitching. Ben gave her an enquiring look. 'I've just been interviewed by Ke ... by DCI Harris,' she said. 'I'm pretty sure he suspects Mrs Haughan, possibly with the collusion of Martin Morris, the gardener-handyman who discovered the body, but I believe he's barking up the wrong tree. I was thinking of doing a little quiet nosing around when he's not looking. It occurred to me ...' Quite deliberately, she left the idea hanging in the air.

Ben took several slow draws on his cigarette. Leaning forward with his elbows on his knees, his head lowered, he reminded Melissa of an elderly dog cautiously sniffing the ground. 'I take it you'd like me to join you in a bit of off-the-record sleuthing,' he said at length.

'Something like that.'

'What did you have in mind?'

'We're agreed that Haughan was a nasty piece of work. There must be others with a motive for killing him.'

'And how do you propose to set about finding them?'

'That's where I hoped you'd be able to help. Don't you journalists have some sort of unofficial information network?'

'We have contacts, yes,' he said guardedly, 'but we have to have something to go on. Tell me what you know so far, and I'll see if there's any way I can add to it.'

Melissa repeated the account she had given Harris. Ben pulled a notebook from among the debris on the floor and began scribbling in shorthand, occasionally interrupting to clarify a point. When she had finished he closed his eyes for a few seconds. Then he opened them and said softly, 'Haughan was a prize bastard, wasn't he? I'm almost tempted to say, "Good luck, hope you get away with it," to whoever did it.'

'I'm worried that the wrong person will be charged,' said Melissa.

He shot her a keen look. 'Any particular reason?'

She was silent for a moment, trying to decide whether to confide in him. At last she said, still uncertain whether she was doing the right thing, 'There's something I didn't mention to DCI Harris. I suppose I should have done, but ...'

Ben listened with pursed lips while she told him about the fragment of conversation she had overheard and her instinctive reaction to it. 'Well, I agree with you, they don't seem to be in it together,' he commented, 'but that isn't to say that neither of them did the killing. There must be strong reasons why they both see themselves as suspects.'

'It wasn't just what they said ... there was something about Martin's tone that made me sure he was telling the truth. As for Verity ... I find it hard to picture her wielding enough force to hit her husband over the head.'

'It doesn't take a lot of strength, just accuracy,' said Ben drily, 'All the same, I'm inclined to agree with you, but as for Martin ... he's got to be number one suspect until we find someone else with motive. Let's recap.' He put down his pen, lit another cigarette and inhaled, his eyes half closed. 'The wife has a deep-rooted grudge against the husband and she's confided in the gardener. The two of them are sufficiently close for her to fear they might be suspected of a conspiracy. Maybe they've been having a bonk on the side.' Ben gave a sudden, hoarse chuckle. 'Shades of Lady Chatterley, eh?' A lascivious gleam in his eye invited Melissa to share the joke but, remembering Verity's distress, she managed only the faintest of smiles. 'Go on,' she said.

'Morris has been up to something that makes it "look bad" for him.'

'Not necessarily "up to something",' Melissa corrected him. 'It's safe to assume that he had a grudge against Stewart which might be construed as a motive for killing him, but not that he's done anything about it.'

'All right, point taken. But whatever it is, it's enough to scare the pants off him ... and he's told Verity enough to scare her rigid as well.'

'I've just had a thought,' said Melissa suddenly. 'Those messages ... we've been thinking that all we have to do is find out who sent them and we've got our killer. Supposing they came from someone else?'

Ben frowned. 'I don't follow you.'

'Someone – let's suppose it was Martin – has been sending them to Stewart just to give him some aggro. He – or she, it could be a woman – finds opportunities to slip them in among the papers in the office. Word gets around. Someone else, someone who's planning to murder Stewart, hears about it, realises that he's not the only one with a motive and calculates that, when the body is found, the police will be hunting for the writer of the poems.'

'A ready-made red herring, eh?' mused Ben. He thought for a moment, then shook his head and smiled. 'Possible, I suppose, but a bit far-fetched. Might do for one of your books, Mel, but ...'

'It's worth considering,' Melissa protested. There was a shade of condescension in his manner that nettled her.

'Okay, we'll bear it in mind. Let's think about the messages themselves. How many people had the opportunity to plant them?'

'From what I've heard, pretty well everyone who works here and the students as well. People seem to wander in and out of the office at will.'

Ben stubbed out his cigarette and set the ashtray down on a teetering pile of books, 'I'd like to have a peek at them. You say you have copies?'

'In my room. I'll go and get them.' Melissa got up and opened the door. Outside, the breeze was blowing even more strongly, sending dead leaves skittering across the gravel. Among them was a screwed-up scrap of paper. Instinctively, she picked it up and smoothed it out. Ben heard her exclamation and came to look at it over her shoulder. The three typewritten lines read:

> Despair drove out hope
> Hope's death be on your conscience
> This day, hope shall die

'Another one?' said Ben.

'Yes. Stewart must have dropped it as he went out to try and catch whoever had left it.' A sequence of pictures flashed into her mind: Stewart, disturbed by an unfamiliar sound, leaping out of bed, hastily pulling on some clothes and dashing downstairs, finding yet another missive, flinging open the door and rushing outside, screwing up the paper and dropping it as he ran. He must have gone charging out like a bull at a gate while his killer lurked in the shadows, awaiting his chance to strike. Was that how it had happened?

She studied the scrap of paper again. 'Notice the choice of words?' she said. "Hope *shall* die'. Not will, shall. It's not just a prediction, it's an edict ... almost the pronouncement of a sentence.'

Ben gave a soft whistle. 'Maybe your red herring will turn out to be a shark,' he said thoughtfully.

CHAPTER THIRTEEN

'We'd better hand this over to the police,' said Melissa. 'There's loads of them still here, doing a fingertip search in the orchard.'

'No rush,' said Ben, who was already copying the latest missive into his notebook. 'Let's look at them all together and see if we can find a pattern.' He picked up the sheet of paper on which Melissa had jotted down the earlier messages. 'Is this the lot?'

'As far as I know, these are the only survivors. There were several earlier ones that were destroyed.'

'What about the one pinned to the effigy?'

'That wasn't a poem.' Melissa thought for a moment. 'I'm not sure of the exact words … "The death of hope is nigh", or something similar.'

'Makes a change from the end of the world being nigh, I suppose. Any idea where it is now?'

'I imagine the police have it. I never thought to take it – I was too busy calming Verity and theorising about the effigy itself.'

'Pity. We could have made some comparisons. They were probably all done on the same machine, but no doubt the forensic boys will be checking that.' Ben studied the one they had just found. 'I'd say this was done on a portable. A fairly ancient one, by the looks of it. Is there one like that in the office?'

'I've no idea.'

'No problem, we can soon check.'

Together, they studied the four short stanzas in silence for a few seconds. Then Melissa said, 'There's a definite change of mood in these last two, isn't there? The references to hope … I wonder if that meant something to the victim that he didn't mention to anyone else? And "Hope's death be on your conscience" – that does suggest a revenge killing, doesn't it?'

'By someone who didn't understand Stewart Haughan very well,' said Ben drily. 'From what you've told me, and what I've seen for myself, he had about as much conscience as Winnie the Pooh had brains.'

'That might not have been apparent to everyone. He had charm as well and he could turn it on like instant sunshine,' said Melissa, remembering the dazzling smile that had accompanied his outrageous denial that he had ever accused his wife of planting the messages. 'I'd say he was capable of putting on any act and doing almost anything that suited his purpose. If anyone got hurt that was their hard luck – I doubt if he'd even notice.'

'A typical psychopath, in fact. It doesn't always lead to acts of violence,' Ben explained, seeing her look of surprise. 'At least, not physical violence – it can show up in lots of ways. I wonder if, somewhere along the line, something he did resulted, directly or indirectly, in the death of a young woman?' His expression brightened as inspiration struck. 'A young woman called "Hope", perhaps?'

Melissa shook her head. 'I thought of that. I asked if he'd ever known or employed anyone by that name, but he was quite definite he hadn't.'

'That needn't mean a thing. He could have been lying, or – if Hope had become troublesome, or maybe pregnant – he could have dumped her and then emptied his memory of the whole episode. That's how a psychopath's mind works.'

Melissa gave him a curious glance. 'You've made a study of them?'

'Did a bit of research once for a feature I was writing.' Ben frowned momentarily, as if recalling something unpleasant. 'Let's get back to Haughan. What do we know about his background?'

'All I know is what he told me over dinner last night.'

'Let's have it, for what it's worth.' Ben indicated the armchair and picked up the kettle. 'Want another mug of Strickland's Special?'

'Not just now thanks. I may want to drive presently.' Melissa sat back in the chair and closed her eyes, reliving that ghastly evening. 'He was boasting about how he'd devised this brilliant new learning system he calls CRALLS – your brain absorbs the information while your hands are busy performing some creative task. That's how he himself began learning foreign languages. He boasted that the system was his idea from start to finish, but Verity claims the initial inspiration was hers. She's responsible for all the creative crafts taught here.'

'Sounds as if she had more than one reason for holding a grudge,' Ben commented. 'Why did he want to learn foreign languages, by the way?'

'Before setting up this Centre five years ago, he was a marketing executive for a firm in London. His boss put him in charge of European sales.'

'Any idea what firm it was?'

'I think he said they made bathroom and shower fittings.' Melissa pressed a hand to her forehead. 'He did mention a name … something to do with water … 'clearwater', 'watershed' … does that ring a bell?'

"Headwaters'?' suggested Ben.

'That's it! You know them?'

'Only too well.' He spoke with what sounded like a touch of bitterness. 'So, he was a marketing type. A ladies' man, no doubt, full of charm and bullshit for all occasions. Chat up the receptionists, screw the purchasing managers' secretaries …' Ben broke open a fresh packet of cigarettes, his mouth curling in contempt.

'It could well be,' Melissa agreed. 'As I said, he had the kind of sledgehammer charm that would knock an impressionable woman silly. Maybe one of his conquests from that period took him seriously ... ruined her life over him, wrecked her marriage or broke off her engagement ... maybe some jilted husband or fiancé has at last caught up with him. Is something wrong?' she added.

'No. Why?'

'You were giving me a strange look.'

'Was I? Just thinking about what you were saying. You reckon some jilted lover's been plotting murder for five years or more?' Ben went over to the window and stood with his back to her, drinking coffee and staring out. For a minute or two he was silent, apparently deep in thought. 'It's a hell of a long shot,' he said at last. 'Besides, how could the killer get close enough to plant these messages ... if they are connected with the killing? We still don't know that for certain.'

'Someone who came here on a course – sent by their employer, maybe. He recognises the name of the proprietor, realises it's the man who ruined his life ... he'd probably have several weeks' notice ... that would give him time to plan ...'

Ben drained his mug, swung round and put it back on the tray. His movements were slow and deliberate, his brow knotted above his deep-set eyes. He used his spent cigarette to light a fresh one before crushing the stub in the ashtray. 'It's a fascinating theory, but to follow it up would take days, maybe weeks, of detective work.' He met Melissa's eager gaze with a weary smile. 'Sorry, Mel, I think you'll have to let old Deadpan get on with it – he's got the resources.'

'You disappoint me. I thought you'd jump at the chance of pipping him at the post.'

'I agree, it would be fun – but where do we start? Even if we confined our enquiries to people who were here at the relevant time, it could run into a dozen or more. We'd have to get lists of students, find out who they work for, check whether any of those firms had been customers of Headwaters while Haughan was one of their reps ... it's not practicable, Mel, can't you see that?'

'I suppose so,' she admitted glumly. It had seemed such a brilliant idea. Then she had another brainwave. 'What about the Headwaters staff? Maybe the connection is there? Stewart's former secretary, for example … couldn't you at least find out through one of your contacts …' She broke off, aware that she was beginning to sound emotional.

'You really feel strongly about this, don't you?' he said gently.

'Yes, I do. I'm a woman, I can understand something of what Verity has suffered … I don't believe she had any part in her husband's murder, but I can see why Ken Harris suspects her. She's been through enough hell already … if I could turn up something to lead the police to the real killer … surely there's something we can do.'

'I suppose I could get someone to make one or two enquiries into Haughan's London past,' said Ben, after another pause. 'All right, you're on. I might chat up that dolly bird in the office as well – Sadie, isn't it? – see what I can pick up there. How about you? I take it you're going to do your share of ferreting around.'

'This may sound pointless, but I'm going to try and find out a bit more about haiku,' said Melissa, whose thoughts had begun running on another track, now that she had gained her point. 'From what I remember, it's a form with very precise rules. If I could talk to a person who's really familiar with it, I might get an idea. My friend Iris knows someone – I'll have a word with her. You never know, the messages may contain clues that wouldn't occur to an outsider.'

Ben shrugged. His own knowledge of haiku went no further than recognising the name and he was plainly not prepared to attach any significance to the anonymous writer's use of the form.

'Would Haughan have been likely to spot clues, even if they were there? He doesn't seem to have been the type to go in for poetry.'

'No, but he might have spotted a connection with something in his past that had nothing to do with poetic form. All right,' she agreed, getting to her feet. 'I know you claim that psychopaths can empty their memories when it suits them. I know it's a long shot, but it's bugging me and I shan't rest until I've followed it up. She picked up the scrap of paper that had triggered their discussion. 'I'd better take this and hand it over to whoever's in charge of the search party. Good hunting!'

'You too!'

There was a payphone on the ground floor of the main building, tucked away beneath the massive oak staircase. At the far end of the impressive entrance hall was a fireplace with a surround and overmantel made from one solid piece of stone, beautifully carved with flowers and classical motifs. Above it hung an early painting of Uphanger, flanked by portraits of a jovial gentleman with ruddy cheeks and white whiskers and a serene-looking lady in a lace fichu and frilled cap. The original owners, perhaps – Verity's ancestors? As she waited for her call to be connected, Melissa pictured the hall as it might have been at Christmas long ago, with bright rugs on the flagged floor, a log fire blazing and lights glittering on a tall tree surrounded by gifts. The kind of picture to gladden the heart of a child. Verity's child, who had not lived to see it.

There was a click, and ringing tone for a few seconds, before she heard Iris's brisk 'Hullo!'

'Iris, it's Melissa.'

'What's wrong?'

'What makes you think …?'

'Heard it in your voice.'

'You're right … but I can't explain now.' Despite the fact there was no one within earshot, Melissa spoke in a low tone. 'Iris, you remember that book you lent me about haiku? What was it called?'

'Haven't a clue. I'll look it up if you hang on.'

'You mean, you still have it? I thought you'd borrowed it from someone at college.'

'I did. Took it back every week for ages. Never saw the chap again. Didn't bother too much – only a thin paperback. Maybe he had another copy.'

'Will you lend it to me again?'

'Sure. What's going on?'

'Be with you in half an hour. I'll tell you then. Bye.' As Melissa replaced the receiver, a door at the far end of the hall opened and Martin Morris appeared, apparently making for the office. She stepped forward to intercept him.

'How is Verity – Mrs Haughan – now?'

'She's still shocked, of course, but the doctor has given her a sedative.' He hesitated for a moment before saying, 'Would you mind going to see her? I know she wants to thank you for being so … sympathetic.'

'Yes, of course.'

'If you go through that door,' – he indicated the way he had just come – 'you'll find yourself in a passage leading to the private quarters. She's in the kitchen.'

Melissa found Verity at an ironing board, with a wicker basket of laundry on the floor beside her. In the strong sunlight that streamed through the end window, she looked paler and more fragile than ever, the iron almost too heavy for her small hand.

'Are you sure you feel up to doing that?' said Melissa.

'It has to be done. Mrs Lucas isn't in this week. Stewart said, with only two guests, we didn't need her. He said we might as well save the money. He always liked to save money. It was because of saving money that Tammy died.' Her mouth crimped and tears oozed from her eyes as she blindly pushed the iron to and fro.

'Leave it for now.' Gently but firmly, Melissa took the iron, stood it on its heel and pulled out the plug. 'Why don't you send for Mrs Lucas – you can't cope on your own. There's the business to look after as well.'

'You're right. I'll get Peggy to call her.' Wiping her eyes, Verity went to the telephone and pressed the button to call the office. When Peggy answered she gave the instruction and then added, 'I'll be coming to talk to all the staff after lunch. Say at half-past two – will you tell them?' She put down the telephone and turned to Melissa. 'You've been so kind … I just wanted to thank you.'

'Anyone would have done the same. If there's anything else I can do, just ask.'

'I mustn't impose on your time. You're a guest, here to get on with your writing.' A subtle change had come over Verity; she was calm and composed, almost businesslike. 'Now, about lunch …'

'There's no need to worry about me. I can get something at a pub.'

'No, no, you must have it here … you've paid for it. And dinner … you and Mr Strickland … Mrs Lucas will see to it, if she can come, otherwise I'll manage. I insist,' she added, as if to counter any further objection.

'All right, thank you,' said Melissa. Despite Verity's appearance of fragility, she detected a steely resilience beneath the surface. 'I'm going out now, but I'll be back in time for lunch.'

'So, what's all this about?' demanded Iris as she led the way into the kitchen of Elder Cottage.

'Stewart Haughan – the proprietor of Uphanger Learning Centre – has been murdered,' said Melissa.

Iris's eyes and mouth rounded in astonishment. 'Good heavens! When?'

'Some time early this morning. And guess who's in charge of the investigation?'

'Your own PC Plod? The one you went there to dodge?' The look of consternation changed to one of impish glee. 'He's been checking on you. Rang me last night. Didn't admit to knowing where you were, but he guessed. No flies on that one!' Still grinning like a Cheshire cat, Iris filled a kettle, put it on the stove and took out three of her hand-painted mugs.

'No coffee for me, thanks,' said Melissa. 'It's coming out of my ears already. And you can take that smirk off your face,' she added crossly.

'No offence,' said Iris, unabashed.

Melissa pulled a chair from under the table and sat down. Immediately, Binkie, Iris's fluffy half-Persian, who had stood expectantly watching from the moment she entered, sprang to her lap and settled down, purring in ecstasy.

'Aah, bless him, he loves his Auntie Mel!' crooned Iris. 'Just me and Gloria for coffee, then.' She glanced up at the ceiling as a series of bumps and the whine of a vacuum cleaner overhead spoke of the activities of their cheerful, energetic domestic help. 'Bet Ken's eyes popped when he saw you there. What did you tell him?'

'The truth. I'll tell you the whole story some other time, but I've been over it twice already since breakfast and my head's buzzing.'

'Any idea who did it?'

'Ken seems to think the gardener and Haughan's wife are having an affair, and that he did the deed, possibly with her connivance.'

'And Madame Melissa Poirot disagrees, I suppose?'

'Well … yes. And Ben has his doubts as well.'

'Who's Ben?'

'A journalist – another 'writer in retreat' who arrived this morning.' As briefly as possible, Melissa recounted their deliberations, finishing with her own conviction that the key to the mystery lay in the haiku messages. 'That's why I want to re-read that book,' she explained. 'It's a pity you lost touch with the chap who lent it to you … I'd like a talk with him.'

'Funny you should say that.' Iris went to the dresser and fetched a thin volume with a pale green paper cover on which the title *The Joys of Haiku* was printed in mock oriental characters. 'He's written his name at the back. Never spotted it before – only looked in the front. Here.' She handed the book to Melissa. Inside the back cover was written in pencil, 'M. Dunmow', with an address in Cheltenham.

'Oh, fine.' Melissa slid the book into her handbag. 'When I've finished with it, I could return it for you. I'm sure to be going to Cheltenham one day next week.'

'Thanks. Time he had it back. So, what's this place like?'

'Beautiful. I brought one of their brochures for you to see, by the way.' Melissa fished it from her handbag and put it on the table. Iris picked it up, flipped idly through the pages, put it down again and glanced at the clock on the wall, which showed a couple of minutes past eleven. 'Coffee's ready. Better call Gloria.'

The cottage shook as Gloria's substantial frame trundled down the narrow staircase. She came bouncing into the kitchen, her round, rosy face registering surprise and pleasure at seeing Melissa.

'Ooh, Mrs Craig, I thought you was away this week!' she exclaimed. She settled her ample behind on one of Iris's rush-seated chairs and reached for a nut cookie. Her eye fell on the Uphanger brochure. 'This where you're staying?' She studied the cover with interest. 'It looks lovely.' She began turning the pages, pausing at one showing a photograph of a beaming Stewart Haughan in the centre. Arranged in a semi-circle below it were smaller portraits of Verity, Peggy, Pam, Sadie and two other women whom Melissa did not recognise, but guessed were the language teachers.

'I knows that one.' Gloria jabbed a plump forefinger at one of the faces. 'She were in hospital with my sister. Peggy someone.'

'Peggy Drage,' said Melissa. 'She's Mr Haughan's secretary.' She was about to add 'the late Mr Haughan', but changed her mind.

The prospect of repeating the story yet again for Gloria's benefit was too much. Iris could tell her later.

At the moment, however, Gloria was preoccupied with medical details. 'Had a hystree-otomy,' she said between slurps of coffee.

'I think you mean hysterectomy,' suggested Melissa.

'Thassit.' Gloria smacked her lips and repeated the word with relish. 'Real upset she were, and so were her Dad. Never had no kids, and now she never will. She were crying buckets one day when I were visiting and her Dad were trying to comfort her.'

'Poor woman,' said Melissa softly. 'I can imagine how she must have felt. She's still quite young.'

'Mm.' Gloria, herself the mother of three thriving youngsters, nodded sympathetically. She finished her coffee and stared reflectively into the empty mug. 'Shouldn't be surprised if some bloke had let her down,' she said. 'It's the sort of thing they do, innit? Her Dad should've gone and sorted him out.'

Melissa pushed back her chair. 'I must be going. Thanks for the loan of the book, Iris. You'll go to my house tomorrow as usual, Gloria?'

'Course I will.' Gloria waved from the sink, where she was rinsing out the coffee mugs. 'See you next week.'

'Dunmow,' repeated Melissa to herself as she reversed the car and set out on her return journey to Uphanger. 'Now, where have I heard that name before?'

CHAPTER FOURTEEN

'I wonder what Mrs Haughan's going to talk to us about,' said Pam, her eyes on the computer monitor. 'If she wants to know about the bookings, I can tell her they're pretty healthy and so are the finances. I'm just running off a summary.' She pressed a key and the printer began chattering and disgorging paper covered in figures.

'Maybe she'll start by giving us all a wage increase, to encourage us to carry on in the face of adversity,' said George. 'I don't think,' he added with a sneer.

'I hardly think her first concern will be money,' said Pam reproachfully.

'Why not?' George, seated at his desk in an alcove surrounded on three sides by shelves stacked with books and audio cassettes, swung round in his swivel chair. '*His* usually was.' He jerked his head in the direction of their late employer's office door, just as Peggy emerged with an armful of manila folders. 'Hullo, what've you been up to? Looking for the last will and testament? I don't suppose there'll be anything in it for you!' He gave a sardonic chuckle as he swung back, uncovered an elderly typewriter and inserted an index card.

'It's the stuff from his pending tray,' explained Peggy, with a weary glance at the back of his head. There were times when she found his waspish sense of humour hard to take. 'Contracts and things he's been negotiating. I thought I'd see where everything's got to before this afternoon's meeting, so that I can put Verity in the picture.' She sat down at her desk and opened the first folder.

Sadie, who had been quietly putting papers into a filing cabinet, came across to Peggy's desk, her young face alight with curiosity.

'Do you want any help?' she asked hopefully.

Peggy shook her head. 'Not with these, thank you. They're all highly confidential.'

'I daresay the police will want to go through all his private stuff,' said Pam.

'Oh dear, do you think so?' Peggy clasped the folder to her chest as if protecting it from prying eyes.

'Sure to.' George glanced at her over his shoulder, his eyes gleaming with malice behind his glasses. 'They'll be looking for evidence of some jiggery-pokery that might suggest a motive for killing him. It'll be like the Robert Maxwell investigation – no stone will be left unturned!' He whipped the card from the machine and flourished it like a banner. 'Well, they're welcome to rummage through this lot. There's nothing suspicious here – unless you count the CRALLS crap. That's a con from start to finish, but the fools turn up and pay for it, so who am I to knock it?'

'It's a very clever system,' insisted Peggy. 'He was very proud of it.' Her throat tightened as she spoke and she gave the file in her hands an angry shake, as if it was somehow responsible for the emotion that threatened to spill out. She swallowed hard and said, unconsciously quoting from the brochure that Stewart himself had written, 'It's the cornerstone of the business.'

'Someone told me that the original idea was Mrs Haughan's,' said a new voice. Ben Strickland was standing on the other side of the counter. 'Sorry, couldn't help overhearing that last bit,' he apologised.

'Who says so?' asked Pam curiously.

'I picked it up on the grapevine.'

'No, you're mistaken,' said Peggy earnestly. 'Verity's craft lessons are an important part of the programme, of course, and she helped him in the development stages, but Stewart ...' She broke off and bit her lip, conscious that her eyes were smarting, terrified of making a fool of herself.

'I was wondering if anyone could let me have some change for the telephone,' Ben held out a couple of one pound coins. 'I've got several calls to make.'

'There'll be some in the petty cash,' said Peggy. 'George, would you mind ...'

'Sorry, I'm busy,' said George without turning round. 'Sadie can do it.'

Sadie was only too willing to oblige. She came skipping across the office, her blonde curls bouncing. She bent down behind the counter and came up with a cash box, took Ben's money and replaced it with a handful of small change, counting each piece aloud in a chirpy, nasal voice. 'The payphone's over there,' she said, pointing with a raspberry-pink-tipped finger.

'I know, I've been here before.' Ben gave an ingratiating smile. 'But you weren't here when I gave my creative writing course, were you? I'm sure I'd have remembered *you*.'

Sadie beamed in response to the implied compliment. She had wide blue eyes, pearly teeth and dimples like the young Shirley Temple. 'No, I wasn't,' she replied coyly. 'I started at the same time as George – a couple of months ago. But he's only part-time – I'm full-time, same as Peggy and Pam,' she added proudly, glancing towards the alcove, where George sat hunched over his card index. 'I got the job through Youth Opportunities,' she went on. She was evidently a compulsive giver of confidences to strangers. An ideal subject for an investigator, in fact.

'This must have been a dreadful shock to all of you,' Ben remarked conversationally, leaning an elbow on the counter like one settling down for a chat. 'The sort of thing you read about in the papers, only happening to other people, eh? I don't suppose you heard or saw anything suspicious?'

'There was those funny poems,' Sadie began, only too ready to take the bait, but before she could say another word Peggy called out, with a reproving glare at Ben, 'Hurry up and finish that filing, Sadie, I'm going to need your help with the post.'

'Forgive me. Mustn't hold up the good work.' Ben straightened up, gave a mock salute and ambled away, his footsteps echoing on the stone floor.

As soon as he was out of earshot, George leaned back in his chair and muttered, without turning his head, 'Better be careful what you say in front of him. He's the press, don't forget, even if he is off duty. A lot of sensational publicity won't do the place any good.'

In the small dining-room where DCI Harris had carried out his interviews, Mrs Lucas, a slight, grey-haired woman in a flower-printed overall, served Melissa and Ben with bowls of home-made soup and crusty bread warm from the oven. They sat opposite one another at the circular table which, like the dresser on the wall facing the window, was an antique piece of dark, solid-oak with a patina that reflected many years of regular waxing. On the floor was a rich Turkey carpet and the dresser shelves carried an assortment of old china plates and ornaments that the most up-market dealer would not have been ashamed to display in his showroom. Melissa reflected that the room had been furnished by someone with money and taste. Verity's family's money and her taste? This was her inheritance. Was that why Stewart had married her? And was she, perhaps, not entirely sorry to be free of him?

'Penny for 'em,' said Ben between spoonfuls of soup.

'I was just admiring the decor.' She did not want to think the thoughts that had come into her mind, much less share them with Ben.

'Yeah. Mrs H isn't hard up for a bob or two – unless this place is mortgaged up to the hilt, of course. In which case, there'd most likely be life insurance to cover it.'

Mrs Lucas spared Melissa the need to reply by coming in to collect the soup plates and put a slab of Double Gloucester cheese and a bowl of salad on the table.

'How is Mrs Haughan?' asked Melissa.

'Bearing up very well, all things considered,' the woman replied in her warm Gloucestershire accent. 'Mind you,' she went on, lowering her voice. 'I don't like to speak out of turn, but it isn't as if he's been the best of husbands. Just the same, it's been a great shock, of course. We're all very upset.'

'I'm sure you are,' said Melissa.

'Did you make that soup?' asked Ben, with apparent carelessness. 'I did.'

'I guessed as much. Best I've ever tasted.'

Mrs Lucas beamed. 'I made the bread as well,' she said. Ben saluted her with the slice that he had been spreading with butter before sinking his teeth into it. 'Superb!' he said, chewing with gusto. 'I reckon Mrs Haughan's very lucky to have your help.'

'I do what I can. She needs all the help she can get, poor love. I'll just go and make you some coffee.' Still smiling, Mrs Lucas withdrew, then popped her head round the door to say, 'Grilled lamb steaks for dinner.'

'Yum!' Ben smacked his lips, then, as the door closed, lowered his voice and said to Melissa, 'I must have a chat with Mrs L presently. I'll get more out of her than the office staff. The only one willing to gossip is the youngster, and she's only been here five minutes. So's the old grouch who skulks in the corner. The secretary seems to be running the show for the time being. Bit of a dragon, that one. Upset at the boss's sudden departure though, kept on sniffing.'

'I heard she had a hysterectomy recently. That would tend to make her a bit emotional.'

'How did that come up?' he asked. Melissa reported Gloria's hospital visit. 'And that's all you've got to show for a morning's sleuthing?' His grin held gentle mockery, but no malice.

'I've got hold of a book on haiku. I'm going to study it after lunch.'

'Big deal. We're halfway to cracking the case already.'

'There's no need for sarcasm. What have you come up with?'

'Not a lot, but there's one thing I want to follow up. That gardener chap – incidentally, he's comparatively new as well – I've seen him somewhere before. I'll try and have a chat with him during the afternoon.'

'He's an architect by profession, if that's any help. I imagine he's working here because he couldn't get anything else.'

'I don't recall interviewing any architects lately.' Ben ruminated over the last crust from Mrs Lucas's wholemeal loaf. 'I'll bet Haughan got him on the cheap, like his part-time pensioner and his trainee office girl. He must have been a real tightwad.' Ben pushed back his chair and stood up. 'See you at dinner.'

'Aren't you going to stay for coffee?'

'No thanks. I brew my own, remember?'

He went out, whistling the chorus of a number from 'Kiss Me Kate'. What a great show that was, thought Melissa, then sat bolt upright in her chair. *Kate!* The memory bounced up in her mind like a jack-in-the-box. In all the excitement, the snatch of conversation she had overheard on her arrival at Uphanger had slipped from her memory.

She was on the point of calling Ben back to tell him about it, then remembered his good-natured teasing and decided not to. She'd show him he wasn't the only one capable of turning up a clue or so. For what it was worth, she'd follow this one up herself.

CHAPTER FIFTEEN

It was almost four o'clock when Melissa, absorbed in her study of *The Joys of Haiku*, heard a tap at her door. She opened it, expecting to see Ben; instead it was DCI Kenneth Harris who stood outside, hands raised in mock defence.

'I haven't come to hassle you, I just came to thank you for handing over the latest bit of evidence,' he said. 'Any chance of a cup of tea?' he added, with his eyes on the kettle.

'Come in and I'll make you one.' She filled the kettle and switched it on, while Harris lowered his bulky frame on to a chair. 'What did you make of it?'

'It's gone to forensics for comparison with the others.'

'The message itself, I mean.'

'It looks like the culmination of a sort of war of attrition the killer's been waging against Haughan. We've got a psychiatrist at work, building up a profile of the killer – he's been given the text of all the poems. We're waiting to see what he makes of them. Have you managed to pick up anything else?'

'Not a lot. Stewart Haughan used to work for a firm called Headwaters that makes bathroom fittings – but I expect you know that already.'

'Right.'

'And Ben Strickland – I believe you've already met my fellow "writer in retreat" – gave a creative writing course here back in the summer. He says that from what he saw then, Haughan was the bluff and hearty type to anyone useful to him and a prize bully to his underlings.'

'Yes, I knew all that too. I also know Ben from way back. Could have made a name for himself as a political journalist if he'd kept off the booze.'

'I've noticed he likes a tipple, but I didn't realise he had a serious problem.'

'Took to the bottle after Ann – his wife – died in a car accident some years ago. Not a complete alcoholic ... just the occasional bender that made him unreliable. He's made something of a comeback lately though, doing special enquiries, uncovering malpractice and corruption.' Harris gave a gravelly chuckle. 'He's been a bit of a thorn in our flesh from time to time.'

'So I gather. He seems quite proud of it. Here's your tea.'

'Ah, thanks!' Harris took the mug that Melissa handed him and drank thirstily.

'Don't gulp it down when it's hot, it's not good for you,' she reproved him.

His eyes met hers over the rim of the mug. 'How nice to know you care!' he said, with mock intensity.

'Speaking of Ben,' she said, ignoring the jibe. 'Did you know he was a substitute for me? I was invited to give that course, but Haughan wouldn't pay a decent fee. It would be interesting to know what he did fork out,' she added reflectively. 'Quite a bit less than Ben was worth, I expect – and he made him wait for it.'

'I understand they agreed on a modest fee plus four days here to work on his book,' said Harris. 'Poor old Ben – it was the best he could squeeze out of the old tightwad, as he called him. Everything I've heard about the deceased so far points to a man universally – and justifiably – disliked. Apart from the secretary, who seems an emotional type who'd boohoo over the death of a mouse, no one seems particularly cut up, not even his wife.'

'He treated her pretty badly. Did you find out if they had a child, by the way?'

'Yes, they did – a little girl who died about seven years ago. The gardener – Morris – knew that, by the way, although he didn't know any details. So he says. Reading between the lines, the widow seems to have confided in him quite a bit. Cosy little chats over the compost heap, that sort of thing.'

'Ken, what are you suggesting?'

'We – Sergeant Waters and I – have a strong hunch there's something cooking between the artistic Mrs Haughan and her handsome gardener. Nothing definite as yet – in fact, the received wisdom in the office is that he fancies the girl who does the accounts. We think that's an impression he's given deliberately, to hide his real feelings. And we also believe Morris is an assumed name.'

'What makes you think that?'

'He didn't produce any documents or a national insurance number when he started work here and the local DSS have no record of him. He's supposed to be an architect, but the name doesn't appear in the Institute records, not even as a student member. According to the secretary, Haughan engaged him on a casual basis – accommodation in the caravan in exchange for a few hours' gardening a week and a few pounds to keep him in food. Morris, as he calls himself, said he wanted P and Q to work on a thesis for his doctorate. I gather Haughan didn't bother to ask too many questions – just got his wife to make the caravan habitable.'

'The fact that he was getting his services on the cheap was enough for him, no doubt,' said Melissa bitterly. 'It must have suited him down to the ground. What about the machine used to type the poems, by the way? Any progress on that front?'

'We've taken specimens from two machines in the office. Both are quite old and both have elite type, but without a detailed comparison we can't say for certain whether either was the one used. We'll have to wait and see. What about you?' Harris picked up *The Joys of Haiku*. 'Found any poetic clues yet?'

'You'll probably pooh-pooh this, but I think I may have stumbled on something.' She picked up the sheets of paper on which she had written the text of all the messages that she had seen. 'Look, there's a very definite change of style in the latest ones. They stick to the five-seven-five syllable count, but in other respects they don't seem to conform to the … the universal *spirit* of haiku. There, I knew you'd sneer,' she added, seeing his indulgent smile.

'I'm not sneering,' he assured her. 'What's your theory?'

'I think they may have been written by two different people, one who understands haiku and one who knows only the basic structure. The later ones break several traditions, like not using the same word more than once, for example. And the underlying menace – haiku is all about nature and the seasons, beauty, sorrow, things of the soul …' Melissa broke off, aware that she was beginning to sound sentimental.

'Which points to what?' Harris prompted gently.

'It was common knowledge that Haughan had been getting those messages over a period of several weeks. Suppose the killer decided to send a few of his own? Suppose he's familiar enough with haiku to get the form right, but hasn't grasped the philosophy. He'd bank on the supposition that the police would assume they all came from one source and concentrate on tracking down the original writer.'

'Hmm.' Harris appeared to consider. 'It's an interesting thought, but pretty far-fetched. It's more likely that he simply decided to begin on a low note and then step up the psychological pressure. It could be someone with a long-standing score to settle who wanted to have a bit of fun with the victim before moving in for the kill.'

'That suggests a pretty sick mind,' said Melissa with a shudder.

'It does, doesn't it?' Harris put the book back on the desk and stood up. 'And there's another thing you should take on board, for your own safety.'

'Whatever do you mean?'

'I know you and your passion for poking your nose into mysteries and I don't want you getting it bloodied or worse. This isn't for publication at the moment, but the post-mortem showed that Haughan wasn't killed by that blow on the back of the neck.'

'He wasn't?'

'No. He died of suffocation.'

'I don't understand.'

'The killer used the blow to the head first to render the victim unconscious. In some cases, that causes immediate death, but it can't be relied on. A pad or something similar held over the nose and mouth for a couple of minutes, to block off the air supply, makes absolutely certain.'

'How horribly cold-blooded. What does it tell us?'

'It tells us we're looking for a professional killer – possibly someone with commando training. Someone very dangerous indeed. So leave the detective work to us from now on unless you want to run the risk of getting similar treatment.' For a moment, Harris dropped his professional tone; he put his hands on her shoulders and gazed earnestly into her face. 'Please remember what I say, Mel. You mean a lot to me, you know.'

'Yes,' she replied quietly. 'I know. I'll be careful.'

'I must be getting back to the station. Thanks for the tea.'

'You're welcome.'

When he had gone, she went outside. After a cool and blustery morning, the wind had dropped, the clouds had dispersed and the air was warm and still. There was no one about except a couple of uniformed policemen guarding an area of the orchard sealed off by blue and white plastic tape. Remembering what she had seen there, she averted her gaze and went round to the front of the house, where she stood for a while to enjoy the brown, green and gold patchwork of fields and woodland. Presently, she sat down on one of the benches placed on either side of the entrance, leaned against the wall and closed her eyes, enjoying the sun on her face and the comforting warmth of the stone on her back. She could hear the high-pitched calls of swallows and house martins as they circled overhead in their ceaseless search for insects, packing their tiny bodies with the food they needed to sustain them on their flight back to Africa. Bees buzzed among the flowers; from the distance came the rhythmic clank of a harvester. All was seemingly peace and order, yet beneath the gentle harmony of the season ran a discordant undertow of hatred and vengeance that, only a few hours ago, had claimed the life of a man.

In her novels, Melissa regularly wrote of dark secrets and hidden suffering ruthlessly brought to the surface by the fallout from a single, apparently unrelated, act of violence. Today she had seen the harsh reality; today she had learned of human pain which should have remained locked away: Verity grieving over the death of her child and Peggy for the children she could never bear; Ben ruining a promising career by seeking in drink relief from the anguish of bereavement. Then there was the mysterious Kate, still to be identified. Why had George Ballard suggested there might be some link between her death and the haiku messages? It was time to find the answer to that question. She got up and went into the house.

As she entered the hall she almost collided with Sadie, who had a bundle of letters in one hand and a shapeless bag, apparently made out of sacking, dangling from a shoulder. 'Oops!' she said, dodging aside. 'Got to hurry to catch the post.' She scuttled out of the door and disappeared; a few seconds later, through one of the mullioned windows facing the drive, Melissa saw her on a bicycle, pedalling at a dangerous pace towards the gate. A long-case clock in the hall struck five.

Melissa went to the counter and looked into the general office. Peggy was there alone, pushing papers into folders. When she saw Melissa she said, 'Is there something you want?'

'Actually, I wondered if I could have a private word.'

Peggy regarded her warily. 'What about?' she asked.

'I don't want you to think I'm poking my nose into your late employer's affairs,' Melissa began. 'I wouldn't be doing this, only before he died, he asked me if I'd try to find out who had been sending those poems. He was very worried about them, you know, even though he pretended not to be. He showed some to the police, but they refused to take him seriously.'

'I know,' said Peggy curtly. 'Verity told us this afternoon. They're taking them seriously now all right.'

'I imagine they've been questioning all of you.'

'They have. We couldn't tell them anything. We don't know anything. No one saw the messages being planted. Some of the early ones came by post, but we never kept the envelopes. It's a total mystery.'

'Have you any theories of your own?'

Peggy appeared startled. 'Me? What makes you say that?'

'The day I arrived, I heard you discussing the messages with your colleague, Mr ... I didn't get his name.'

'George Ballard. What of it?'

'You mentioned a girl called Kate, who worked here some time ago.'

Peggy nodded. 'That's right. About eighteen months ago. She was only here for a few weeks.'

'Why did she leave?'

Peggy lowered her eyes and fiddled with the papers on her desk. 'She ... didn't get on very well with Stewart.'

'Did she leave of her own accord?'

'Not exactly. She was on a month's trial and she wasn't really up to the job, so Stewart said he couldn't take her on permanently.'

'Was she very upset?'

'I don't know. I suppose she might have been. No one likes to be sacked, but it happens, doesn't it?' Peggy pushed a sheaf of papers into a folder and disappeared into what had been Haughan's office.

Melissa had a strong impression that this was her way of ending the conversation; it was an impression that was confirmed by Peggy's expression on finding her still there when she returned.

Melissa affected not to notice the latent hostility. 'Do you know if Kate got another job after leaving here?' she asked.

There was a long pause before Peggy said, with evident reluctance, 'She couldn't have done. She went into hospital.'

'What was wrong with her?'

'She had some sort of breakdown.'

'Because Haughan had sacked her?'

'No … at least …' Peggy was looking more unhappy by the minute. She clasped and unclasped her hands, picked up files and put them down again.

'At least what?' Melissa persisted. 'Peggy, you must tell me. You might know something that could lead us to Stewart's killer.'

'You think so?' At these words, Peggy's manner changed completely. It was as if a bottle of effervescent liquid had been uncorked; the words rushed out like foam. 'She'd already had treatment for a breakdown following the death of her boyfriend in a car crash, but nobody here knew that, nobody understood the effect it would have on her, losing her job like that. The doctors didn't realise how bad she was either, they thought she was responding to treatment. Then one night she wandered out of the building and disappeared. They found her body the next morning.' Peggy covered her eyes. 'I … we … felt dreadful.'

'Are you saying that nobody here knew anything at all about her history?'

As suddenly as the barrier had lifted, it fell again. 'Not at first,' Peggy muttered.

'But the accident must have been reported in the press.'

'Pam remembered something.' The words came out in a series of spasmodic jerks. 'She got concerned … at the way Stewart … I mean, at the way Kate reacted … when he snapped at her. It was just his way … we tried to explain … he was like that with all of us at times.'

'Did anyone tell Stewart what she'd been through?'

Peggy nodded miserably. 'Yes,' she whispered. 'I did. I asked him to be a bit more gentle with her.'

'And what was his reaction?' As if I couldn't guess, Melissa added to herself.

'He said she had to go at the end of her trial period. It wasn't his fault if she couldn't stand the pace,' Peggy went on desperately, almost as if she were pleading his case. 'He had a business to run, he couldn't afford passengers …'

For a moment, Melissa thought she was going to burst into tears. She waited for a moment to give her a chance to control herself, then said gently, 'You've worked for him for a long time, haven't you?'

Peggy nodded. 'I was his secretary in London, before he started the Learning Centre. We – he and Verity and I – built it up together.'

'Is Verity going to carry on with the business?'

'She says so. We're all going to do our best to help her make a go of it.'

'I hope you're successful.' Melissa was on the point of leaving, then remembered that there was something else she wanted to know. 'That girl, Kate – what was her surname?'

'It was quite unusual … it began with a D. Dunmow, that was it. Kate Dunmow.'

CHAPTER SIXTEEN

Kate Dunmow. Now she remembered the case. The discovery of the body. The sensational reports, picking over the bones of the earlier tragedy that had caused her breakdown. Allegations that she had been discharged from hospital too soon, left to fend for herself before she was fit. Her readmission when she was unable to cope. Merciless criticism of the hospital authorities for inadequate supervision. How, the media vociferously demanded, could it happen that a patient in their care was able to wander off into the bitter, numbing cold of a January night and not be missed until it was too late? A representative of the hospital staff blamed lack of resources; a local MP demanded a public enquiry.

Kate Dunmow, in a state of acute depression after losing her job at Uphanger Learning Centre, had taken her own life. Some eighteen months later, the man who had sacked her had been murdered, after receiving threatening messages written in the form of haiku poems. Into Melissa's hands had come a book on haiku belonging to a man whose name was also Dunmow. Working at Uphanger was a man who was thought by the police to have given an assumed name, who was believed to be having an affair with the victim's wife, who in turn appeared to have enjoyed little in the way of love or respect from her late husband, who was a man for whom no one, apart from his secretary, had anything good to say … the progression went on and on, like a grim parody of a nursery jingle.

There had been a telephone number as well as an address inside the back cover of *The Joys of Haiku*. Melissa hurried back to her room, found it, returned to the house and tapped out the number on the instrument in the hall. There was a short spell of ringing tone, then a click as an answering machine the other end was switched on. 'This is Maurice Dunmow,' said a voice that sounded familiar. 'I'm sorry I can't take your call at present. Please leave a message, or during office hours you might catch me on ...' There followed a Cheltenham number, which Melissa repeated in her head as she replaced the receiver. It was almost half-past five; the office was probably closed, but it was worth a try.

'Good afternoon, Fletcher and Crispin,' said a tartly impatient female voice at the end of the wire.

'Is Mr Maurice Dunmow there, please?'

'Who's calling?'

'He won't know my name. I have a book that he lent to a friend of mine and she asked me to return it. He's not answering his home number and I wondered if ...'

'Mr Dunmow is on sick leave,' interrupted the voice.

'Do you know when he's expected back?'

'I've no idea.'

Plainly, Fletcher and Crispin did not bother to train their employees in the art of public relations, thought Melissa as she mechanically thanked the woman and hung up.

It wasn't certain that she had recognised the recorded voice. She would never be able to swear to it. On its own, it meant nothing. Taken with the other bits of circumstantial evidence – and that was all they were, at the very most, circumstantial – it might be significant, but otherwise ... How many innocent people had been suspected, charged, even convicted, on circumstantial evidence? In her head, she could still hear the voices of Verity Haughan and Martin Morris, hoarse with fear as they discussed their predicament: '*I didn't kill him. I swear it,*' and '*They'll say I had a motive ... think it's some sort of conspiracy*'. On the one hand, an emotionally battered wife; on the other, a man out to avenge the death of a relative. An unholy liaison between the two? The tabloids would have a field day.

Melissa left the booth in a mood of deep depression. At the same moment Peggy emerged from the office and, without a glance in her direction, left through the front door. A stillness fell over the wide hall, emphasised rather than broken by the sonorous ticking of the long-case clock. Melissa went across to the counter. The room behind it was empty, the desks cleared, the typewriters and other office machines shrouded in their plastic covers. The light filtering through the mullioned and leaded windows was grey and oppressive.

During the past half-hour, clouds had built up over the sinking sun. An air of gloom hung over the place; as Melissa stepped outside, the first drops of rain made dark splotches on the gravel. She hurried round the house towards the guest wing, noticed the light in Ben's room and without stopping to think, tapped on the window.

He held a glass of red wine in one hand as he opened the door. From the flush on his face, she guessed it was not his first.

'Ah, Madame Sherlock Holmes! Or should I say, *Miz* Sherlock …?'

'Just say Melissa,' she interrupted him. She was not in the mood for anti-feminist jokes of the weaker sort.

'Yes, Ma'am!' He stood to attention, transferred the glass into his left hand and gave a soldierly salute. 'Have a drink!'

'It's a bit early, but I think I will – thanks.'

'You'll have to use my tooth glass – it's quite clean.' He vanished into the bathroom and returned with a small tumbler. 'So what's eating you?' he asked, as he poured from a bottle of supermarket claret.

'Who says anything's eating me?' She took a mouthful from the drink he handed her, then another. It made her feel a little better, but not much.

'Don't dissimulate, woman,' said Ben as he topped up his own glass. 'You look as if you put your shirt on a nag that ran backwards.'

Melissa smiled ruefully. 'In a way, I suppose I have.'

'Tell Uncle Ben.'

Briefly, she did so. As soon as she mentioned the name 'Dunmow', he snapped his fingers. 'That's it, you've got it!' he exclaimed. 'Now I remember where I met the chap who calls himself Martin Morris. He was visiting his sister in a psychiatric hospital at the time I was doing a feature on treating mentally ill patients in the community. He was just leaving – off to take part in some Territorial Army exercise, as I recall – so we only exchanged a few words.'

'He's in the Territorials?' said Melissa. Her heart was sinking fast. 'Do they learn ...?' She broke off, remembering Harris's injunction not to reveal the precise cause of Haughan's death.

Ben had shrewdly read her thoughts. 'Commando tactics? They don't get trained to SAS standards, if that's what you mean, but an experienced TA officer would have picked up enough to sneak up on someone and render them unconscious with a well-aimed blow to the head.'

Chesterton's words ran through her head: *I bring you naught for your comfort.* Already, she could see Martin – or Maurice, as she must now think of him – sitting in the dock, with Verity beside him as an accessory.

'Are you absolutely sure about this? Have you actually spoken to him?' she asked, dismally aware that she was clutching at a paper straw.

Ben gave a short laugh. 'Haven't had a chance, have I? He's not been around all afternoon. Maybe he remembers me and is keeping out of my way.' He gulped the last of his wine, smacking his lips. 'Reckoned without the Strickland RAM, didn't he?'

'You could be mistaken. It must have been a fair while ago.'

'Soon after the accident to the girl's boyfriend, I imagine. It was the trauma that caused her first breakdown. About two years ago – I can soon check.'

Melissa paced about the small room, sipping her wine and thinking aloud. 'Kate Dunmow came to work here about eighteen months ago, so she'd been having treatment during the six months before that. At some time after leaving the hospital, she found this job. She couldn't stand Haughan's bullying, he gave her the sack, and within less than four weeks she was back in hospital. Two weeks after that, she killed herself.'

'And big brother blames her nasty boss for not showing a little more consideration and understanding. He must have been brooding, plotting revenge ever since.' Ben went to replenish their drinks, found the bottle empty and dumped it on the floor. 'Bugger. Have to open another.'

'Not for me,' she said hastily.

'Ooh, a one-glass drinker, eh?' he taunted.

'Before dinner, yes. Besides, I want to keep a clear head. I want to think.'

'Not much thinking to be done, is there? A series of anonymous messages, low-key at first but unmistakably – with hindsight – referring to Kate Dunmow's death. The pressure steps up, probably after brother Maurice gets his job here and can watch the effect for himself. Then the final phase, thinly veiled threats before he moves in for the kill.' Ben contemplated his drink, nodding his head as the pieces of puzzle slotted together. 'Looks as if our friend Deadpan Harris is on the right track after all, doesn't it? Are we going to tell him, or let him find out for himself?'

'I'm not going to tell him,' said Melissa miserably. 'It's all circumstantial, there's nothing to prove that Maurice Dunmow killed Haughan.'

'You're kidding yourself, m'dear. He did it all right. Where's that sodding corkscrew?' Ben rummaged among the chaos of his filing system. 'Ah, got it!' He sat down with a bottle on the floor between his feet and set about opening it. 'Think I might tell Harris,' he said ruminatively. 'Be fun to shoot the old bugger's fox, wouldn't it?'

'This isn't my idea of fun,' she replied shortly. His lack of sensitivity grated, to say the least, although she supposed that any journalist would be bound to develop a thick skin in time. Besides, he too had had his share of personal tragedy. She watched him as, having peeled off the foil cap, he prepared to tackle the cork. 'Why don't you leave that till later?' she suggested. 'It's time to think about getting ready for dinner.'

He looked up quickly and for a moment she thought he was going to make a sharp retort. To her surprise, he put both corkscrew and bottle aside and stood up. 'You're right,' he said, his voice unexpectedly gentle. 'And try not to worry too much about Dunmow. With a good lawyer, he'll get away with a fairly lenient sentence.'

'You think so?'

'Can't be sure, but when the jury learn what kind of animal Haughan was …' Ben's eyes seemed to glaze over for a moment. He swayed a little and put an arm round Melissa's shoulders – to steady himself, she suspected, rather than out of sympathetic concern. 'Don't you go losing any sleep over it.'

'What about Verity?'

For a moment, Ben looked nonplussed, as if he had barely considered the widow's possible role in the affair. Then he said confidently, 'She'll be okay – so long as the prosecution don't call Mrs Lucas as a witness,' he added, with an exaggerated air of mystery.

'Why do you say that?'

'I went back to help with the washing up while Mrs H was giving her troops a pep talk. The old duck was only too ready to enlarge on her opinion of Haughan. You know how their little girl died?' Melissa shook her head. 'Meningitis. She was taken ill while they were on holiday in France. Tightwad hadn't taken out medical insurance and wouldn't shell out for a French doctor. By the time they got the kid back to England and into hospital, it was too late.'

'So that's what Verity meant when she implied that Stewart's meanness caused Tammy's death. Poor woman – she'll never have forgiven him for that.'

'Exactly. She'd better keep *stumm* or the prosecution will go to town on her.'

'Suppose Mrs Lucas mentions it to the police?'

Ben gave a harsh laugh. 'She won't say anything that might lead the police to the killer. She says Haughan got what he deserved – except she thinks a short, sharp shock was too good for him. And let me tell you one thing,' he went on, and for a moment his voice wavered. 'She's ab–so–lutely right. If anyone deserved boiling in oil, it was that bastard.' There was a fierce intensity in his expression; his eyes seemed more deeply embedded than usual in their sockets. A shiver ran down Melissa's spine.

'Yes … well, I'll be going now. Thanks for the drink,' she said, and let herself out.

It was almost, she thought as she let herself into her own room, as if he too had had a score to settle with Stewart Haughan. On the other hand, of course, it might simply have been the effect of guzzling too much wine too quickly.

CHAPTER SEVENTEEN

It would not have surprised Melissa if Ben had skipped dinner, but at half-past seven he tapped on her door to ask if she was ready. Apart from a slightly heightened colour, he showed no sign of his earlier carousing and his manner was perfectly normal.

'I'll leave your dessert and the coffee percolator on the sideboard for you to help yourselves,' said Mrs Lucas as she ushered them into the dining-room. She brought a series of covered dishes from a heated trolley and set a carafe of red wine on the table. 'I'll be off in a minute to get supper for my family, but I've told Mrs Haughan I'll be here first thing in the morning to give a hand.'

'Those look absolutely superb!' exclaimed Ben as she removed the lid from a dish of grilled lamb steaks. 'Mrs Haughan has every reason to give thanks for your sterling qualities, both as a cook and as a friend,' he went on, with a gallant little bow.

'I'm sure I'm only too ready to do *anything* to help her,' Mrs Lucas replied. 'You can depend on it,' she added with a conspiratorial air as she left the room.

Remembering the artless smiles that Ben's lunchtime compliments had evoked, Melissa asked, 'What was all that nudge-nudge, wink-wink about?'

'I warned her against saying too much about how things were between Haughan and his wife,' Ben explained. 'Remembering your concern that Mrs H shouldn't be involved,' he added casually, 'although I'm afraid there's bound to be talk about her and Dunmow ... come on, don't let this get cold.' He broke off to help himself to food. 'Want some plonk?' He picked up the carafe and sniffed at it cautiously. 'This seems okay.'

Melissa held out her glass. 'I'll try some, thanks.'

He poured her drink, tilted the carafe over his own glass, then grimaced, put it down and picked up a jug of water.

'Better stick to this for now,' he said. 'Going out presently for a drink with … someone.' The hesitation was barely perceptible, but Melissa pricked up her ears.

'Anything to do with our enquiries?'

'What enquiries? I thought we had it sewn up.' He picked up his knife and fork and began eating.

Melissa was tempted to raise the subject of his animosity towards Haughan, so forcefully expressed only a couple of hours ago, but decided not to. It might be prudent to pretend she had not noticed. He might not even remember what he had said. He had been pretty drunk at the time – but not *that* drunk, she reflected, or he wouldn't be sitting here now, tucking into food. Just enough to make him momentarily careless.

He finished his dessert and stood up, glancing at his watch. 'Got to leave you, I'll skip the coffee,' he said, and left without further explanation.

Perhaps he was going to meet DCI Harris, in which case, Maurice Dunmow's days – probably hours – of freedom were numbered. Melissa's spirits sank to a new low as she went to the sideboard to help herself from the percolator. She sat down again and moodily stirred cream into her cup, resting her chin on her free hand, her mind an uneasy jumble of conflicting facts and impressions.

Common sense pointed unwaveringly at Maurice Dunmow's guilt. He had motive, opportunity and – if Ben's throwaway remark about his service with the Territorial Army was correct – the know-how. Yet her intuition continued to plead otherwise. Which led her on to a very simple question: if not Dunmow, then who? From what she had heard, the people with a grudge against Haughan were legion.

On that basis, Ben was now a suspect. With the best part of a bottle of wine inside him, he had dropped his guard to reveal strong personal feelings against the murdered man. That in itself meant very little. He was, by all accounts, one among many, although the fact that he had appeared on the scene on the morning of the crime set him apart from the others ... and he, too, had done service in the army. And why had he come to Uphanger in the first place? To support the business of a man whom he heartily disliked seemed illogical, to say the least.

There was a tap on the door and Verity entered. 'Have you finished?' she asked. 'Was everything all right?' Her loose blouse, worn over a full skirt, seemed to accentuate her air of fragility, but her manner was composed, brisk, almost businesslike.

'It was fine, thank you,' said Melissa. 'Mrs Lucas is a wonderful cook. Let me help you clear away.' She half expected the offer to be declined, but Verity took two trays from the sideboard and handed her one.

'Would you care for a liqueur?' she asked when they had carried everything into the kitchen and loaded the dishwasher. 'I'm going to have one,' she went on, as Melissa hesitated.

'All right, just a small one, thank you.'

Verity's hand shook slightly as she poured two glasses of creme de menthe. She handed one to her guest, took a seat at the table and gestured at the chair facing her. 'Do sit down.'

'I understand from Peggy that you plan to carry on with the business,' said Melissa.

Verity nodded and a spark of animation lit up her pale features. 'It's the only way I can afford to keep this place up, and I couldn't bear to leave it. I'll be able to use some of my own ideas, branch out in some new ways. Stewart would never let me have any say in policy.'

Melissa raised her glass in salute. 'I wish you every success.'

'Thank you.' For a minute or two, Verity sat looking at her own glass, fiddling with the stem and making no attempt at conversation. Then she said abruptly, without raising her eyes, 'The police think Martin killed Stewart, don't they?'

'I'm afraid he's the chief suspect at the moment.'

'I'm sure he didn't do it,' said Verity flatly. 'He swears he didn't, and I believe him.'

'I think I do as well.'

Verity looked up in surprise. 'You do? But why? You hardly know him. What is it to you?'

'I can usually tell when someone is speaking the truth,' said Melissa simply, and went on to recount what she had overheard. 'I didn't say anything to the police at the time, but I've since learned that he had a very strong motive,' she added. 'And I'm afraid that when the police discover his real identity ...'

Verity's eyes stretched and her mouth fell open. 'You know about that?' she whispered fearfully.

Melissa nodded. 'And I know what happened to his sister.'

'Are you going to tell the police?'

'No, but Ben Strickland intends to. He seems quite convinced of Martin's – or should I say, Maurice Dunmow's guilt.'

'How did you find out his real name? Did someone tell you? Does anyone else know?' The staccato questions followed one another like a burst of rapid fire. In an attempt to damp down the rising panic, Melissa kept her manner deliberately matter-of-fact as she explained about finding the address and telephone number in the poetry book.

'He hated Stewart, he said he'd been toying with the idea of killing him for what he did to his sister,' Verity said miserably. 'He told me everything ... how he'd been planning to do it ... and then someone else did it and he realises now that he wouldn't ... he could never actually kill anyone, not even Stewart... but he's terrified no one will believe him.' Her agitation was mounting; her hands, nervously fingering the glass, were never still, her voice was jerky and tremulous and her eyes flickered to and fro. 'He's had some sort of army training,' she went on. 'I suppose that'll go against him too.'

'He sent the haiku poems, didn't he?'

'The early ones. Not the last one, or the effigy. He was utterly shocked when he heard about that.'

'I noticed he seemed startled when I mentioned it. And thinking about it after studying the book on haiku, I feel sure the poems were written by different people.'

'That's exactly what Martin said must have happened.'

'I doubt if the police will take that view,' said Melissa, remembering Harris's reaction to that very theory. 'If they consider it at all, they'll probably argue that it was a deliberate ploy to put them off the scent – and goodness knows what a jury would make of it. What made him begin his campaign anyway? Looked at rationally, it does seem a bit futile.'

Verity made a resigned gesture with her free hand. 'I agree, but he hasn't really been in a normal state of mind since his sister's death. It was a terrible blow to him. The two of them were pretty much alone in the world – both their parents were killed in a plane crash several years ago. He felt he couldn't cope, his work suffered and he was living on tranquillisers. He started writing the poems as a kind of therapy and then had the idea of sending them to Stewart – hoping to prick his conscience, give him a sense of guilt, he said.' She gave a short, scornful laugh. 'He didn't realise that Stewart doesn't ... didn't know the meaning of guilt or conscience.'

'What brought him here?'

'He saw our advertisement for a gardener-cum-handyman and came after it. He admits that hounding Stewart was becoming an obsession and he wanted to be on the spot to see the effects of his 'campaign', as he calls it. He got his doctor to say he was suffering from nervous exhaustion and sign him off work for three months.'

'How long ago was that?'

'About two months.'

'When did you suspect that he was the one sending the poems to Stewart?'

'You may find this hard to believe, but Stewart never said a word to me about the poems until last Friday. He hardly ever confided in me. And it was only this morning, after he found the … found Stewart's body, that Martin admitted what he'd been doing. He was in such a state that he blurted out the whole story.' Verity began fiddling nervously with her hair. 'We each had a brandy to steady ourselves and agreed to say as little as possible to the police. I'd say I slept through the whole thing – which was true, by the way – and he'd simply tell it like it happened. We knew there'd be further questions later on, but we couldn't see any further ahead then … and Martin was in deep shock. He needs help, you know.' Her eyes pleaded for compassion and understanding.

'If he's charged, the magistrate will almost certainly call for psychiatric reports,' said Melissa. 'I'm more concerned about what he may tell the police about you. You'd confided in him, hadn't you? Told him how you blamed Stewart for Tammy's death?'

Verity's composure, which had become increasingly fragile, suddenly disintegrated altogether. Her face crumpled and she gave a strangled sob. The stem of her glass snapped under her convulsive grip and she sat for a moment staring in stupefaction at the blood oozing from her finger.

'Here, let me look at that,' said Melissa.

'It's all right, it's nothing.' Verity jumped to her feet, went to the sink and held the wound under the cold tap. Her shoulders heaved and her breath came in uneven gasps as she fought for self-control. Melissa went to her and put an arm round her shoulders, amazed at how slight and insubstantial her body seemed. 'I'm so sorry,' she said gently. 'I didn't mean to distress you, but you have to face the fact that things don't look good for you.'

'I know.' Verity buried her face on Melissa's shoulder and sobbed for several minutes. At last she became quieter, dried her hand with a towel and wrapped a handkerchief round the cut. Her face was still working and her breathing spasmodic as she asked, 'Who told you how Tammy died?'

'You hinted at it yourself – remember? – and Mrs Lucas told Ben Strickland the full story!'

Mechanically, Verity put the broken glass in a waste bin, fetched a cloth and wiped the table. Then she sat down and put her face in her hands. 'Oh God, what a mess!' she groaned. 'He's a journalist – it'll be in all the papers.'

'Not through Ben. He's even warned Mrs Lucas about repeating what she told him. He believes Martin – Maurice Dunmow – killed Stewart, but neither of us wants you to be involved.'

'Thank you.' Verity reached across the table and gave Melissa's hand a squeeze.

'I've been trying to figure out some other line of enquiry,' said Melissa.

'You sound like a police officer.' Verity gave a wan smile.

'I've had some experience of how they talk,' Melissa admitted, with an irony that went over Verity's head. 'Obviously, someone else hated Stewart … Ben himself seems to have done, but I don't know why.'

'Him and God knows how many others,' said Verity bitterly.

'Would that include you?' The question slipped out involuntarily; its effect was startling.

Verity took a deep breath and looked directly at Melissa. The change in her appearance was almost frightening; her smoke-blue eyes had become hard as marbles and her voice, normally low-pitched and melodious, took on a harsh note as she said, 'My God, how I hated him! But I've had to hide it all these years, haven't I? "Don't rock the boat Verry", "We must keep up appearances for the sake of the business, Verry". And always penny-pinching, always doing things on the cheap …' She clenched her fists until the knuckle-bones threatened to break through the flesh.

'Why didn't you leave him?'

'And lose my interest in Uphanger? Uncle Joshua was totally taken in by Stewart, like I was, and he altered his will to leave it to us jointly. That's why Stewart married me, of course – I didn't realise it at the time. I thought he was in love with me, doing the honourable thing because I was pregnant.' She gave a mirthless laugh. 'If it hadn't been for the chance of getting his greedy paws on Uphanger, he'd probably have told me to have an abortion, like he did Peggy.'

'Peggy?' Melissa was thunderstruck. 'He got her pregnant? When?'

'It was while we were living in London and he was still at Headwaters. She was his secretary there and because she's so efficient and speaks foreign languages he asked her to join us in this venture. She'd have done anything he wanted, she was so much in love with him – still is, I suppose, in a dog-like sort of way.'

'Did their affair go on after you came down here?'

'You must be kidding! That would have been too close to home – Stewart didn't believe in fouling his own nest. I don't know where he's been doing his bonking these past few years – he didn't often bother me, that was all I cared about. And I'm glad he's dead, but I had absolutely nothing to do with it.' It was as if a kind of Pandora's box had opened, releasing the pent-up misery of years. 'Whoever did it deserves a medal, but *it wasn't* me!' She drummed her fists on the table like one possessed.

'Shh, calm down. I believe you, but I'm not the one you have to convince,' said Melissa. 'You say Stewart made enemies, but can you think of anyone at all … never mind how long ago it was … who might bear that sort of grudge? Some woman he treated particularly badly, for example?'

Verity's mouth curled. 'He treated them all badly. He'd grow tired of them and drop them. I do remember one in particular, though … one who wouldn't let go so easily. She even got hold of our phone number at home and rang him there. I took the call.'

'Did she say who she was?'

'She said her name was Ann. I thought it was someone from the office and called Stewart to the phone. Then I heard him shouting at her to stop pestering him. I don't know what she was saying to him, but I heard him say something like, "All right, go ahead, see if I care".'

'Do you know if he heard from her again?'

'Not at home, certainly. He was very grumpy for a day or two after that, but that was nothing new. He was quite mercurial in his moods. One minute he'd be a monster and the next he could be all sweetness and light.'

'Did he ever discuss her with you?'

'Not directly, but I do remember something else. I didn't connect the two at the time … maybe there isn't a connection … but a couple of weeks later he was reading one of the morning papers and he suddenly said, 'Well I'm damned! The stupid cow meant it after all!' and burst out laughing.'

'Did he say what he was referring to?'

'No. I asked him, and he said, "Oh, just a bit of unfinished business that's been tidied up", and went off to the office.'

'You didn't find what he'd been reading?'

'He always took the paper to work with him. Anyway, I wasn't that interested.'

'Can you remember exactly when this was?'

Verity thought for a moment. Then she got up and went to look at a calendar that hung next to the dresser. 'It was nine years ago last Sunday,' she said in a faraway voice.

'How can you be so sure?'

'It was Tammy's first birthday. Stewart had forgotten.'

Some time later, when she was back in her own room and preparing for bed, Melissa remembered that Ben's late wife had been called Ann.

CHAPTER EIGHTEEN

It wasn't much to go on, but it was all there was at the moment. A woman called Ann, who had (presumably) been having an affair with Stewart Haughan, tracked him down in his own home and (apparently) threatened some action (unspecified) that she had (possibly) carried out two weeks later.

A string of assumptions, based on hearsay. Verity herself had admitted there was no evidence of a link between the phone call and the news item that had caused Haughan both astonishment and amusement … but supposing there had been? Could it be a story about the death of a woman, someone with whom he had been having an affair but who could not face the fact that it was over? He had expressed satisfaction at the way some 'unfinished business' had been settled; from what Melissa had learned of the man, such a reaction would in those circumstances be entirely in character.

He would be relieved to think he would no longer have to suffer the irritation and inconvenience of being pursued by a lover of whom he had tired. He would have no regrets, no more regard for the woman's pain and humiliation than if she had been a sparrow in flight, broken and tossed lifeless into the gutter by a passing car. He would care still less for the anguish of bereavement suffered by those who had loved her.

Nine years on, Stewart Haughan had been murdered, apparently in an act of vengeance. Someone with a comparatively recent score to settle was under suspicion, but an exploration of the more distant past might bring to light evidence of a much older debt.

Ben Strickland's wife had died in a car accident and her name was
Ann. In an unguarded moment, Ben had revealed a personal hatred
of Stewart Haughan. That was all.

The chance of there being a connection between these facts and
Stewart's murder was, Melissa told herself again and again as she
lay awake in the darkness, remote, hardly worth considering – but
nevertheless, it existed. Added to her own conviction that Maurice
Dunmow, alias Martin Morris, was innocent, it became a possibility that must be investigated. Tomorrow, as soon as the reference
library was open, she would begin her search.

Having made her decision, she fell into a deep sleep and awoke
late. There was no one about when she went across to the house,
but an electric toaster, a pot of freshly brewed coffee and all the
ingredients for a light breakfast were laid out on the dining-room
sideboard and two places set at the table. She ate two slices of
toast, drank a glass of orange juice and some coffee and went back
to her room.

There was no sign of Ben. Presumably he was still asleep. That
was a relief. She had no wish to explain to him where she was
going. She tucked a notebook into her handbag, put on a coat
and went round to the car park. There were two cars there besides
her own, but only her Golf and an elderly Cortina, presumably
Ben's, showed traces of the rain that had fallen overnight. One of
the office staff must have arrived already. As she drove towards the
gate she passed Sadie on her bicycle, her face rosy with the effort
of pedalling uphill. She gave Melissa a cheery wave as she passed.
Another day was beginning at Uphanger Learning Centre.

The assistant in the reference library showed her to a dingy
basement, where bound copies of newspapers dating back to the
previous century were housed on massive steel shelves. An elderly
man in a shabby raincoat and tweed cap, a hearing aid in one ear and
thick glasses on his nose, was perched at one of the old-fashioned

wooden desks, earnestly copying something into an exercise book. He did not so much as glance up when they entered.

'Professor Griggs, a local historian,' explained the assistant. 'He's as deaf as a post, so don't waste time trying to have a conversation with him.' She showed Melissa where to find the year she was looking for and left her to it.

The search took a considerable time because Verity had had no idea which of several national dailies Stewart had been reading, but at last she found what she was seeking – a short paragraph on an inside page of *The Morning Record*:

> A woman was killed in an accident on the A419 in the early hours of yesterday morning. She was the sole occupant of a Ford Escort which apparently hit the crash barrier on a stretch of dual carriageway just outside Swindon before rolling over and landing on its roof in a ditch. The woman, later identified as Mrs Ann Strickland, wife of Record reporter Ben Strickland, had to be cut from the wreckage and was pronounced dead on arrival at the Princess Margaret hospital. Police are investigating the cause of the accident; a member of the rescue services stated that road conditions were good at the time and no other vehicle was involved.

So that was it. Either deliberately or from a moment of carelessness while in a state of blinding emotion, Ben's wife had lost control of her car and died. The pain of bereavement and the subsequent damage to a promising career caused by drinking too much and too often had, all these years later, prompted the sudden, bitter outburst that Melissa had witnessed against the man he held responsible for the wreckage of his life. Did it mean that Ben Strickland had killed Stewart Haughan?

Melissa's hand was unsteady as she copied the brief report and made a note of the date. She felt no elation or excitement at the successful outcome of her search, only sadness that yet more personal grief was about to be dragged mercilessly into the spotlight. She went upstairs, thanked the assistant and checked that she could obtain a photocopy later if need be. For the moment, the simple fact of her discovery would surely be enough to convince DCI Harris that he had more than one suspect to consider. She went in search of a telephone.

Harris was out on a case and the officer who answered Melissa's call seemed unimpressed by her insistence that the matter was urgent. All he would do was offer to pass the message on, if and when the Chief Inspector made contact with the station, and would she care to leave her number? The last thing she wanted at the moment was to return to Uphanger and come face to face with Ben. She badly needed a sympathetic ear; on impulse, she gave Iris's number, went back to her car and set off for Upper Benbury.

The rainclouds had rolled away, unveiling a sky of limpid blue. Nestling side by side under the hill, their stone-tiled roofs damp and glistening in the September sunlight, the two cottages – hers and Iris's – had an air of unruffled tranquillity. The hawthorn hedge and the elder tree after which the respective dwellings had been named were laden with fruit, the bright red haws a gleaming contrast to the swags of dark berries. The valley beyond was splashed with the glowing pigments of autumn; on the hillside opposite, a herd of young cattle grazed, observed with detached interest by Binkie from his favourite niche on a drystone wall.

A bright yellow Fiesta, recently bestowed on Gloria from his stock of guaranteed-genuine-low-mileage-one-careful-owner used cars by her adoring husband, stood before Melissa's front door. She edged the Golf past, half intending to put it in her garage, then changed her mind and parked it alongside the hedge. There was no getting away from it; she would have to return to Uphanger later on, even if only to collect her things.

Iris emerged from her front door before Melissa had time to ring her bell. 'What's up now?' she demanded. 'Not expecting you back till Friday.'

'Let me in and I'll try and explain. I've been doing some research and I'd like your reaction to what I've uncovered.'

'Sounds intriguing.' Iris stood aside to allow Melissa to enter and then led the way into the kitchen. 'Coffee or herb tea?'

'Herb tea would be lovely. I hope I'm not interrupting you …'

'Not a bit. Wanted to work in the garden, but too wet, have to wait till later.' Iris filled a kettle and put it on the Aga. 'Right. Now tell,' she commanded.

'Seems simple,' said Iris when Melissa had finished her story. 'Tell your PC Plod what you turned up and leave it to him. Don't see the problem. You never wanted the haiku man to be the villain … now you've got something on this other guy …'

'Yes, I know. The trouble is … I know this is going to sound awful but … I don't want either of them … I don't want *anyone* banged up for ridding the earth of an animal like Stewart Haughan.'

For the first time in her life, she was seriously considering the proposition that an act of violence directed by one human being against another could on occasion be justified, and she was shocked by the intensity of her own feelings. She got up and began prowling round the little kitchen. 'He cared for nothing and nobody but himself,' she went on, her anger mounting as she reflected on the toll of misery for which Haughan had been responsible. 'He caused at least three deaths – four if you count poor Peggy's aborted foetus – by sheer, callous indifference. He broke Verity's heart, and those of God knows how many other women … and now two decent men, whose lives he also blighted, whom he pushed to the edge of sanity without even being aware of their existence, are going to be pursued and hounded and castigated, and one of them put on trial and condemned ... and their pain and heartache splashed all over the press ... where's the justice in that?' Melissa turned to face her friend with outflung arms and then, to her own astonishment and bewilderment, burst suddenly and violently into tears.

She sank into a chair and sobbed for several minutes while Iris, ever practical, put a box of paper tissues in front of her and sat patting her shoulder until she became calmer.

'Know your trouble?' she said when the storm had abated. 'Too much involvement with murder and mayhem. Think about it, write about it ... and then get snarled up in the real thing. Bad for the system.'

'I don't do it on purpose,' Melissa hiccupped, still sniffing and dabbing her face and eyes with a lump of sodden tissue. 'Some people are accident-prone – perhaps I'm murder-prone.' She looked appealingly at her friend. 'Iris, what should I do?'

'Simple.' Iris stood up, took their cups to the sink and rinsed them. 'Tell the fuzz what you know. They'll find out anyway, sooner or later. Then fetch your stuff from Uphanger, come home and forget it. Not your problem.'

'No, I suppose not.' Wearily, Melissa combed her hair with her fingers. 'As a matter of fact, I did try to contact Ken Harris as soon as I left the library, but he wasn't available. Then I started think-ing – whoever topped Stewart Haughan did the world a favour so why should I help track him down?'

'Can't go along with that,' said Iris flatly. 'Mind you,' she added with a twinkle in her bright grey eyes, 'there's one or two in this village who wouldn't be missed if your commando should pass this way.'

Melissa gave a weak giggle and received an encouraging pat on the shoulder. 'That's better. Hate to see you looking like a wet weekend. Wonder who that is,' she added as the telephone began to warble. She picked up the receiver and after a moment held it out to Melissa. 'For you.'

'Mel? I got your message – are you okay?' It was Ken Harris and he sounded agitated.

'Yes, but I've found out something you should know, something that may help your enquiry into the Uphanger murder,' she began.

'What's that?'

'I know you suspect Martin Morris, but he wasn't the only one with a grudge against Haughan.'

'We know that,' said Harris impatiently. 'Is that all, because ...'

'No, please listen. Ben Strickland hated him because of the way his wife died ...'

'Strickland? Are you telling me you think Strickland killed Haughan?'

'He had a motive, and opportunity, and ...'

'Now let me tell *you* something,' Harris broke in. 'Ben Strickland's body was found behind a hedge this morning by a local farmer.'

'Oh, no!' Melissa felt as if she had been punched in the stomach. 'Oh, Ken, how dreadful! What happened?'

'The first indications are that he was killed in the same way as Haughan.'

It took a moment for the horror to sink in. Then she whispered, hardly aware of what she was saying, 'So Ben was right, it *was* Maurice Dunmow!' Her head reeled, she was spinning in a void, she felt herself falling and slumped against the wall, clutching the receiver with both hands. Iris came to her side and took her arm to steady her.

'Melissa, are you there?' Harris's voice in her ear, sharp and unfriendly, penetrated the turmoil in her brain. 'What was that you said?'

'I … Martin … Maurice Dunmow …' she stammered, hardly able to get the words out. 'It must have been him. Ben said …'

'Who the hell is Maurice Dunmow?'

'He's … Martin Morris.'

There was a brief pause before Harris said, in an ominously quiet voice, 'I'm at Uphanger. You'd better get back here right away.'

CHAPTER NINETEEN

'Exactly when did you first learn that Martin Morris and Maurice Dunmow are the same man?'

For the second time, Melissa faced Harris across the dining-room table. Not her devoted friend and ardent lover, but a grim-faced Detective Chief Inspector, his sergeant at his side, interviewing a witness guilty of withholding vital information. Her heart thumped and her mouth felt dry.

'I suppose … I began to suspect … when Peggy told me about a Kate Dunmow who had died in tragic circumstances after being sacked from Uphanger by Stewart Haughan.' She hardly recognised her own voice, it sounded so shaky and subdued, as if she were a schoolgirl caught out in a particularly irresponsible prank. But this was no prank; despite her glib promise to Harris to 'be his eyes and ears', she had gone off on a wild-goose chase of her own instead of reporting her findings immediately. As a result of this folly, born of her blind, obstinate faith in her own judgment, a man had died. For the rest of her life, she would have to live with that awful knowledge.

'What action did you take?' Harris's voice cut into her thoughts. She forced herself to look him in the eye. What she read there was not encouraging.

'I'd already found the name and address of Maurice Dunmow inside the back cover of that book of poems.' She indicated with a tilt of her head the copy of *The Joys of Haiku* lying on the table between them. 'There's a phone number as well; I rang it and got a recorded message. I couldn't be sure, but the voice sounded like Martin Morris.'

'Then what?'

'The message said to try his office number.'

'Which is?'

'I didn't write it down. The name of the firm is Fletcher and Crispin.'

'Waters.' Harris flicked a glance at his sergeant, who nodded and left the room. He turned back to Melissa. His jaw was set, his eyes those of an angry stranger. 'It might interest you to know that the man who calls himself Martin Morris has not been seen since yesterday morning.'

'Ben said over lunch yesterday that he'd been looking for him, but we had no idea he'd disappeared altogether.'

'Also for your information, a portable typewriter was found in his caravan. We're pretty certain *all* – the emphasis on the word was pointed and deliberate – 'the so-called haiku messages were typed on it.'

So much for her theory about more than one writer. She had been wrong about that too, wrong about everything. Stricken by a sense of utter failure, she had to ask Harris to repeat his next question.

'What did Strickland want with Morris?'

'He said he'd seen him before but he couldn't think where. Later on, he remembered, but I've no idea if he ever had a chance ...'

'Remembered what?' Harris interrupted.

'That he'd met him in a psychiatric hospital in Gloucester, where he – Morris – was visiting a patient, his sister.'

'When did he tell you this?'

'Late yesterday afternoon. I knocked on his door; I wanted to tell him what I'd found out and we ... he offered me a drink and we talked it round.' Slowly, jerkily, she repeated what she could recall of the conversation.

'And so you came to the conclusion that Martin Morris was in fact Maurice Dunmow.' Without warning, Harris thumped the table with his fist. 'Why, in God's name, didn't you inform us immediately?' he shouted. 'Don't you realise that Strickland would still be alive if you had?'

'Oh, I know, I know!' Melissa moaned, her head in her hands. 'I didn't want to believe … I was so sure Martin was telling the truth … I told Ben I couldn't bring myself to betray him … and he said he was going to tell you himself. When he said he was going to meet someone, I thought it must be you … and I got talking to Verity and we both agreed that it looked very black for Martin … Maurice, I mean … but we just didn't want to believe …'

In utter despair, Melissa covered her face with her hands. Her head throbbed and her eyes burned, but they remained dry. The tears would come later.

'What time did Strickland go out?' It might have been her imagination, but Harris's voice seemed to have softened a little.

'I'm not sure. Dinner was at half-past seven and he didn't stay for coffee. Half-past eight, maybe a little earlier.'

'And you had no idea where he went, or who he was going to meet?'

'No. He almost told me and then changed his mind. He'd had quite a bit to drink earlier. I expect that's what made him let out things he probably wouldn't have done if he'd been sober.'

'He wasn't an alcoholic, you know.' Harris momentarily dropped his official manner. 'He overdid it at times, but he had it more or less under control.'

Melissa sensed that in some way the big detective was defending the reputation of someone he had looked on as a friend. A little hesitantly, she asked, 'Did you know his wife had been having an affair with Stewart Haughan?'

Harris looked up sharply. 'No, I didn't. Are you sure of this?'

'Almost certain. That's what I wanted to tell you when I tried to phone you this morning.'

He took a deep breath and appeared to consider before saying, 'You may as well give me the details – ah, there you are, Waters.' He looked round as his sergeant re-entered. 'Take this down, will you?' He turned back to Melissa. 'Go on.'

'Ben seemed to have no doubt that Martin – that is, Maurice Dunmow – must have killed Haughan. In fact, I had the impression that he wanted to believe it. Then I got to thinking that maybe he wanted *me* to believe it. He started going on about what a bastard Haughan was and how he got what he deserved ... it was obvious that he hated the man's guts, although he never said why. Later on, while I was talking to Verity, she told me ...' Melissa continued with her story, trying to explain the reasoning – now so tragically proved fallacious – that had led her to delve into newspaper reports of nine years ago in the belief that they might throw light on Haughan's death. For the most part, the two policemen listened in silence. At the end, after a few questions on points of detail, Harris ordered Waters to get her statement typed in the incident room set up in one of the lecture rooms of the big, rambling old house.

Melissa, feeling utterly defeated, put her head in her hands and began to weep – not the violent, passionate sobs that had earlier overwhelmed her, but quiet tears of desolation. She longed for some word or gesture of comfort from Harris, but none came. She groped for a handkerchief and dried her eyes. 'Is that all?' she asked without looking at him.

'For the moment, yes, but I'd like you to stay here for the time being. I may want to question you again.'

'Ken, I'm so sorry,' she said humbly.

'I could charge you with obstruction, you know.'

Was he being serious, or did she detect a hint of teasing in his voice? Had he forgiven her? After all, she hadn't been the only one who knew about Martin Morris's true identity. Ben could have reported it himself, she'd believed he was going to … no, that was nothing but a paltry excuse, a craven attempt at self-justification.

'I know, I'm sorry,' she repeated. How futile it sounded. A man was dead, she was partly responsible and all she could find to say was 'I'm sorry'. Harris was writing in his notebook and made no response. She plucked up courage to ask, 'What will happen to Verity?'

He did not look up. 'We'll have to wait and see,' he said. Without another word she left the room. She put her head round the kitchen door, but there was no one there. In the hope that Verity had not been arrested, that she was perhaps in the office, talking to the staff, she made her way along the passage leading from the private wing to the main part of the building. The reception and office area was deserted apart from Sadie, who was standing beside an open drawer of a filing cabinet, absorbed in the contents of a folder.

'Hullo, where is everyone?' asked Melissa. Her soft-soled shoes had made no sound on the stone floor and the girl almost jumped out of her skin on hearing a voice. She looked flustered as she shoved the folder back in the drawer and slammed it shut.

'Sorry if I startled you,' said Melissa.

'I didn't hear you coming,' explained Sadie as she came over to the counter. 'I'm the only one here at the moment. It's George's day off – he only does three days a week. Pam's popped into the village to do some shopping and Peggy's gone to Stowbridge to pick up her tickets from the travel agent.'

'Is she going on holiday?'

'Next week, to the Canaries. She needs it too – I've never seen her look so awful, and no wonder with all this upset.' Sadie had regained some of her poise, but her pert, pretty face was blotchy with crying. 'Oh, Mrs Craig, it's so dreadful!' she burst out. 'They've taken Mrs Haughan away. Do the police think she did it?'

'I'm sure they don't, they just want to ask her some more questions,' said Melissa, trying to sound more confident than she felt.

'And poor Mr Strickland ... I could be the last one who saw him alive.' Tears welled from Sadie's wide blue eyes and dripped down her nose. She fumbled for a tissue and scrubbed her face with it, sniffing.

Melissa stared at her in astonishment. 'Sadie, what are you saying? Was it you Mr Strickland was meeting last night?'

'That's right,' Sadie gulped. 'He took me for a drink at the Fleece.'

'Where's that?'

'In Uphanger village.'

'Have you told the police?'

'Course I have,' said the girl, adding, with a show of indignation, 'Nosey lot, wanted to know *why* he invited me. "Why shouldn't he?" I said. "Nothing unusual about a man inviting a girl for a drink and a chat, is there?" I said.'

'It depends what he wants to chat about,' said Melissa with a faint smile. Inwardly, she was seething. Harris already knew who Strickland had arranged to meet and had kept it from her.

'He wasn't after sex, if that's what you mean,' Sadie assured her.

'Was he after anything else?'

The girl hesitated for a moment, affecting to scrutinise with particular care an unopened letter she had taken from a pile on the counter. 'Like what?' she said off-handedly.

'I don't know. Did he ask you any questions?'

'He asked me how I liked the job, and about Youth Opportunities and how it felt to be unemployed. I thought maybe he was going to write something about it in his paper.'

'Did he ask you anything about what goes on here at Uphanger? About Martin Morris, for example?'

'Martin? He never mentioned him. The police think it was him that topped old Huffin'-'n-Puffin', don't they?' For a split second, something like malicious satisfaction lit up Sadie's tear-stained features. 'No one'll miss *him*, bad-tempered old sod.' Her expression altered again as she said sadly, 'I s'pose Martin did for Mr Strickland as well.'

'It looks like it.'

'But why?'

'The police think he knew him and was afraid he'd recognise him and tell them his real name.'

'You mean, he isn't really Martin Morris?'

'No, his name's Maurice Dunmow. His sister used to work here.'

'Mr Strickland never said anything about that last night. Did he know Martin's real name?'

'Yes.'

'He should've told the fuzz. Then maybe he'd still be here,' said Sadie with unexpected shrewdness.

'You're absolutely right. He said he was going to, but he left it too late.' Once again, Melissa felt the weight of her own guilt in the matter. She was about to turn away and go back to her room when something made her ask, 'Sadie, are you quite certain Mr Strickland didn't talk about anything else? Or anyone else? Or ask you to do something for him?' she added, with a flash of inspiration.

At the final question, Sadie's mobile face registered consternation. It passed in an instant, but it had been there. It was plain the girl was hiding something. Melissa glanced round; there was still no one in sight. 'What did he ask you to do?' she whispered.

Sadie licked her lips, from which most of the pink lipstick had been rubbed away along with the tears. 'He thought he was on to something,' she faltered, after a long hesitation.

'What sort of something?'

'Some fiddle that the boss was up to.'

'What was that?'

'Something about phoney ... no, he called them *phantom* students. Foreign students, who put their names down for courses but never turned up.'

'Why would they do that?'

'So's they could come over here and get jobs, he said.'

'Yes, of course!' It could be a lucrative sideline for a man as greedy and unscrupulous as Haughan. No doubt, in addition to the normal fee, there would be a substantial payment that never went through the books. 'Is that what you were doing just now, looking for names of people who registered but never came to the classes?'

'That's right. I know it doesn't make any difference now Mr Strickland's dead ... I mean, he won't be writing his article or whatever he was planning ... but I just thought it'd be interesting to know ... you won't say anything, will you? If Mrs Haughan or Peggy found out I'd been nosing around, I'd be in dead trouble.'

'Don't worry.'

'I did find several ...' Sadie's expression became conspiratorial, but she broke off as the telephone began to ring. 'Excuse me.' She picked up the instrument and, in an artificially refined tone, announced, 'Uphanger Learning Centre, how may I help you? Sorry, what was that? I don't understand ... just a moment, hold on.' She clapped a hand over the mouthpiece and spoke to Melissa in her normal voice, 'Mrs Craig, do you understand foreign?'

'What sort of foreign?' replied Melissa. 'I know French and German.'

'I think it's German. Will you talk to her?' Sadie held out the receiver, her expression appealing. A little reluctantly, Melissa took it.

'Hullo?' she said cautiously.

'*Guten Tag. Sprechen Sie Deutsch?*' asked a female voice.

'*Jawohl. Kann ich Ihnen helfen?*' There followed a request for some explanation of the Centre's programme of courses in business English.

'*Moment, bitte.*' Melissa translated, but Sadie looked blank.

'I don't know about that,' she said. 'She'll have to talk to Peggy. Ask her to call again later.'

'When will Peggy be back?'

'Soon, I hope. I'm ready for my lunch.' Sadie gave a pout. 'Say about half an hour, to be on the safe side.'

Melissa passed on the relevant information, there was a brief exchange of pleasantries and the woman rang off.

'Did you tell her about the boss being topped?' Sadie asked.

'No.' Melissa looked at her in surprise. 'What gave you that idea?'

'You mentioned Mr Haughan and I thought …'

'I never said anything about … oh, I see! When the woman asked what time Peggy would be back, I said 'In about half an hour, "*wir hoffen*" – that's German for "we hope".'

'Oh, I see. Funny, how it sounds exactly the same.'

'Yes, you get quite a few words like that.'

'I wonder why Peggy never said. Perhaps she didn't want us making fun of her beloved boss's name. I wish I was clever and knew languages,' Sadie went on, a trifle wistfully. 'Course, it's easy for her, she was born in Germany.'

'Oh? How was that?'

'Her Dad was in the army out there, so Pam told me. Oh, and speaking of her Dad, you'll never guess what I found out this morning! I took a peek …' Sadie broke off in confusion as Peggy, who had entered silently through the house, appeared at Melissa's side.

As Sadie had suggested, she did not seem at all well; her features were pallid and drawn, and there were shadows under her eyes. From her expression, it was plain she had overheard Sadie's final remarks. Sensing that a telling-off was about to be administered, Melissa withdrew.

At least, she now knew what had brought Ben Strickland to Uphanger, and it had nothing whatsoever to do with the murder.

In fact, she reflected wryly, had Stewart Haughan known that Ben was planning to expose his racket, *he* might have been the one to commit murder. She wondered whether Ben's investigation had been directed solely against Uphanger, or whether it was part of a probe into the covert activities of a number of private educational establishments. In either case, he had obviously intended to pursue it, despite the death of the proprietor.

She was so absorbed in this line of thought that it was several seconds before the significance of Sadie's other remarks struck her. She stopped dead in her tracks as a further question sprang into her head. Sadie had been about to confide something she had recently learned that was in some way connected with Peggy's father. She had been interrupted by the appearance of Peggy herself; thinking back, it seemed to Melissa that the look on the latter's face had been more than mere annoyance at learning that someone had been tittle-tattling about her private affairs. She had appeared disturbed, almost alarmed.

Did she fear that the incorrigibly inquisitive Sadie had stumbled on something she wanted to remain hidden? Was there perhaps a possibility that the secret, if divulged, would hold a clue to the identity of the murderer?

CHAPTER TWENTY

'Keep calm,' Melissa muttered to herself. 'Think it through before sticking your neck out again. Are you sure you aren't snatching at a straw, desperately trying to find something to show you've been right all along?'

She sat at the desk in her room, trying to make shape and order from the jumble of ideas swirling around in her brain. She grabbed a notebook and wrote furiously for several minutes, then sat back chewing her pen, her mind see-sawing between confidence and misgiving.

Was it too far-fetched to be credible? If she put her theory to Ken Harris, would he laugh it out of court? Or rather, shoot it down in flames before she got half-way through, see it as nothing but a pathetic attempt to boost her shattered self-esteem?

But why should he? The more she thought about it, the more feasible it seemed. She should at least put it forward for consideration. She had already been castigated for not immediately passing on vital information – ah, but that had been information in line with Harris's own thinking. Was she likely to receive a pat on the back by casting doubt on his judgment? Hardly. And yet, he wasn't so small-minded as to refuse to consider … perhaps it might be better to try and dig out a few more facts before …

No! She wasn't going to lay herself open a second time to accusations of withholding what she knew. Relevant or not, Harris was going to hear about this. Resolutely clutching her notebook, she went back to the house, where she was intercepted by a harassed-looking Mrs Lucas.

'I was just wondering – will you be wanting lunch?' she said. 'I don't know whether I'm coming or going this morning, what with poor Mr Strickland dead and Martin disappearing, and now Mrs Haughan's been arrested, of all things! I'm sure I can't imagine what that great hulk of a policeman's thinking of – he wants his head examined!'

'He's only doing his job.' Despite her recent treatment at his hands, Melissa sprang to DCI Harris's defence.

'You mean you believe she killed her husband?' Outrage and astonishment jostled for pride of place on the woman's features.

'I don't believe anything of the kind, and I don't think the police do either,' Melissa assured her hastily. 'But they do think she might know more than she's told them about the murder.'

'To protect that young man, I suppose.' Mrs Lucas nodded, her lips pursed. 'Well, I never saw a sign of anything improper between those two, but I can't say as I'd blame her, poor love, being married to that pig. I just hope they won't be too hard on her, that's all.'

'I hope not,' Melissa sighed.

'So, will you have something to eat now? Soup, or an omelette?'

'Whatever is the least trouble. I just want a quick word with someone first. I'll be with you in a few minutes, if that's all right.' I'd better not let on it's DCI Harris I'm going to talk to, Melissa thought to herself as she hurried upstairs, or she might put soap in my soup.

In what had been the incident room, two uniformed constables were busy dismantling equipment and packing it into cardboard boxes.

'What's going on?' she asked.

'You can have this room back now,' one of them explained, evidently taking her for a member of the staff. 'The enquiry is being conducted from headquarters from now on.'

In other words, they've got their man, thought Melissa. Her spirits plummeted. She had a sudden vision of Maurice Dunmow, lying low at home, unaware that his cover had been blown, confident that Verity would not betray him, daring to hope that he might resume his own identity. Soon, if it had not already happened, the nightmare would begin: the knock on the door, the shock of arrest, the caution, the handcuffs, the ignominious walk to the police car under the inquisitive eyes of neighbours and bystanders, the bleak cell and the endless questions ...

'Is there something you want, Madam?' The younger of the two officers was looking at her curiously and she realised that she must have been waiting there with a vacant look on her face for several seconds.

'Yes, actually, I wanted a word with Chief Inspector Harris,' she said.

'Sorry, he's not here. Can I give him a message?'

'Is Sergeant Waters anywhere around?'

'No, they've both gone back to headquarters. Excuse me.' He broke off as a telephone in one corner of the room began to ring. He picked up the receiver, listened a moment and then said, 'Yes, sir. About half an hour.' He glanced across at Melissa, still standing dejectedly in the doorway, and beckoned. 'There's a lady here would like a word with you, sir.' He handed over the instrument. 'The Chief Inspector's on the line,' he said, and went back to his task.

'Ken, it's Melissa. I've just found out ... no, please, listen,' she said in an urgent whisper, sensing rather than hearing his sigh of exasperation. 'Do you remember how the last two or three messages Haughan received made a lot of references to hope, and the death of hope?'

'So what?' he said impatiently.

'It's only just dawned on me. Haughan and the German word for hope, they're homophones.'

'So the killer knew some basic German and was having a little fun with words. Is that all you want to tell me?'

'No, there's more. Peggy Drage speaks German.'

'So do a lot of people. You, for example.'

'Peggy was born in Germany because her father was stationed there *while he was in the army.*' The dramatic stress she placed on the final words had no noticeable effect. All Harris said, with a hint of irony in his voice, was, 'And you reckon Peggy Drage got her father to teach her a few commando tricks so's she could bump off her ex-lover?'

'There's no need to be sarcastic,' Melissa retorted. 'Peggy still loved Haughan, even though he treated her badly. But that's the point; he *did* treat her abominably.' She repeated the story of Peggy's pregnancy and the pressure Haughan had put on her to have a termination. 'Later, possibly as a result of that operation, she had to have a hysterectomy. You know what that means: no more children, in her case, no children at all. Gloria saw her in hospital and said she reckoned some man had let her down. She said how upset she was, *and so was her father.* I remember Gloria saying, "her Dad should sort him out".' There was silence at the other end and Melissa, desperate to get her message across, but anxious not to be overheard, hissed at him, 'Don't you see what I'm getting at? Maybe her father did "sort him out".'

'All right, you've hit on a possible motive why someone close to Peggy should attack Haughan on her behalf. Now explain why that same person should murder a complete stranger strolling home from the pub.'

'Suppose he recognised Ben and believed Ben had recognised him? They'd both done army service – their paths might have crossed at some time. Suppose he'd been in the same pub that evening and followed him?'

'We've interviewed the barman in the Fleece and he was positive no stranger other than Ben himself was in there. He's sure to have noticed if there had been; Tuesday evenings are always quiet. We've traced everyone else and eliminated them; they were all local people. And no one's seen any strangers in the village recently.'

'Was Maurice Dunmow there?'

'No, but he could have watched from a distance until Ben left the pub, and then followed him.'

Melissa was still not prepared to give up. 'Peggy's father visited her in hospital. He must come and stay with her sometimes,' she persisted. 'Can't you find out where he lives and if he's been here recently?'

'I could, if I thought there was any point.' Harris was beginning to sound impatient. 'What about the messages you're suggesting he sent? Does he happen to have an identical machine to the one we found in Dunmow's van ... identical down to a defective capital "H"?'

'If the caravan was left unlocked, he could have ...'

'Melissa,' said Harris wearily, 'I know you mean well, but you're flogging a dead horse. We're pretty sure we've got our man, so drop it and go home, will you?'

'All right, ask your man if he knows the German for "hope",' she snarled, with as much feeling as she could inject into a stage whisper. 'If he doesn't, you've got the wrong one.' And I, she said to herself as she slammed the phone onto its cradle and flounced out of the room, am going to see if I can track down the right one.

When she calmed down, she had to admit that Harris had shrewdly put his finger on some serious weaknesses in her theory. Over the fluffy mushroom omelette that Mrs Lucas cooked for her, she considered them.

The first thing she had to figure out was how her suspect had cottoned on to the business of the anonymous messages. Perhaps

Peggy had spotted Maurice Dunmow concealing one of his haiku poems among Haughan's papers, but decided to say nothing. She was a compassionate woman; she had been the one to intercede with Haughan over his treatment of Kate. She might have kept quiet rather than expose Maurice – Martin, as she then knew him – knowing that it would mean the loss of his job. After all, the early poems had been innocuous enough, even if they did rile Haughan to an unreasonable extent. Maybe, despite her devotion to him, Peggy had derived a certain satisfaction at seeing him subjected to what must have seemed like a little harmless aggravation. Or – here an altogether more sinister element crept into Melissa's musings – supposing she had seen an opportunity for a scheme of her own?

She might have told her father what was going on. Had the pair of them plotted together to avenge the damage that Haughan had done to both their lives, calculating that once the enquiry into his murder started, the trail would swiftly lead to the gardener-handyman? It was possible that they had known all along that he was really Maurice Dunmow, brother of Kate and former Territorial officer. It might have occurred to them that someone with a grievance against the man who had, indirectly, caused his sister's death, would be a natural suspect. Someone who had already expressed his anguish in the form of those sad little poems.

It did not, on the face of it, fit in with Melissa's own assessment of Peggy's nature ... but perhaps she had not realised that the ultimate goal was murder. Or it might simply be another case – and there were plenty on record – of a rejected and humiliated woman finally turning on the man she loved. Peggy would have known about the portable typewriter in the caravan and guessed that Martin had used it to type his poems. If the van was left unlocked when unattended, she could easily have found an opportunity to slip into it unobserved. One visit would have been enough to type several short, prepared messages, to be used at will.

It *was* feasible. Melissa felt her excitement mounting by the minute. Still, there were a lot of things she needed to know. Sadie had been on the point of telling her something about Peggy's father; it was vital to find out what it was. It could be tricky, getting her on her own in the office. Almost impossible, since Peggy had overheard her final remarks and, if Melissa's reasoning was correct, would be anxious, *very anxious indeed …* at this point, an even more frightening notion began taking shape in her head.

Mrs Lucas interrupted her train of thought by coming in with a pot of coffee. While she was pouring, Melissa said casually, 'I suppose everyone who works here lives in the village?'

'Not everyone. Young Sadie does … in Tinker's Cottage, a couple of doors away from me, in fact. Pam lives a bit further out. Her parents have a farm a mile or so away on the Stowbridge Road.'

'What about Peggy Drage? Does she live locally?'

'I'm not exactly sure. Weatherton, I think … or is it Westerton? I once heard her say it's about five miles away. Why do you ask?'

'No special reason. I just thought … getting to Uphanger must be quite difficult in winter, if it snows.'

'It can be very difficult. In a bad year, this place can be cut off until they get the snow ploughs out to clear the lanes.' Mrs Lucas began gathering the used plates and cutlery. 'Will you be wanting dinner this evening?'

'I'm not sure. I might go home – I really don't want to be here by myself tonight.'

'Suppose Mrs Haughan comes back? *She*'ll be glad of company,' said Mrs Lucas. She managed to convey a suggestion of disapproval, as though she considered Melissa's point of view a selfish one.

'Perhaps you're right. I'll wait around for a while.'

'I'll make a casserole. That's easy to reheat.' The woman bustled out of the room.

Back in her own quarters, Melissa decided that the only practical thing to do for the time being was to keep a look-out for Sadie, follow her home and talk to her there. She might leave at any time after five, depending on whether or not she had to catch the post. It was barely half-past one; it was going to be a long and boring afternoon.

At about half-past four, Melissa slipped back into the house through the private wing and upstairs to the room the police had been using, which was on the first floor, at the front of the house. From a window seat she had a perfect view of the drive; no one could leave without her spotting them. As soon as she saw Sadie pedalling towards the gate on her bicycle, she would go straight to her car.

Pam left soon after five o'clock and drove off in her red Metro. Shortly after, Sadie and Peggy appeared together; surprisingly, they were arm in arm. Or rather, Peggy had Sadie by the arm and appeared to be talking to her in a persuasive manner. They disappeared in the direction of the car park; moments later an engine started up and a white Ford Escort sped away down the drive and turned out of the gate, heading away from the village.

Melissa hurried downstairs and out of the front door, waiting for Sadie to appear, but there was no sign of her. After a couple of minutes she went round to the car park. Except for her own car, and Sadie's bicycle propped against a tree, it was empty.

Apprehension clutched at her stomach. She had had only a glimpse of Peggy at the wheel of the Escort and it had not occurred to her that she might have a passenger. Telling herself not to jump to conclusions, Melissa waited for a few more minutes. There was still no sign of Sadie. She checked the bicycle. Perhaps it had a puncture or some other defect, making it unsafe to ride. That was probably it; Peggy was giving Sadie a lift home. But no, the tyres were sound and the brakes functioning perfectly.

By now convinced that something sinister was going on, Melissa hurried back towards the house. As she reached the front door, a taxi drew up and Verity Haughan stepped out.

CHAPTER TWENTY-ONE

Verity sat in the kitchen with her palms pressed against her temples as if she was trying to prevent her skull from splitting apart. The room was warm, but her teeth were chattering and her eyes unfocused.

'Can I get you a drink?' said Melissa. Verity nodded. 'Brandy?' Another nod. There was a half-full decanter on the dresser; Melissa poured a generous tot and put it on the table. Verity groped rather than reached for the glass, took a sip, swallowed, coughed and took another.

Melissa stood by, fuming with impatience. There were things she needed to know, questions to which Verity might know the answers, but this shaken and trembling woman was in no state to cope with anything that smacked of cross-examination. She felt a spurt of anger at whoever had left her to make her way home alone. She sat down beside her and put a hand on her arm.

'Do you feel like talking?' she asked. 'What did the police say to you?'

'They asked me where he was and I told them I didn't know,' Verity replied jerkily. 'They asked me so many times I lost count. Then they went away. When they came back, they said I could go. I asked them if they'd arrested him, but they wouldn't tell me anything.'

'"He" being Maurice Dunmow?'

'Who else?' Still staring blankly ahead, her mouth working, Verity said, 'Melissa, will you stay with me in the house tonight? I couldn't face being on my own.'

'Yes, of course I will, but there's something I have to find out first. It could be terribly important, and it might help Maurice. Perhaps you know the answer.'

'What is it?' Verity's head had been drooping; now she raised it and straightened her bowed shoulders. For the first time, she looked directly at Melissa.

'It's a long shot, and there may be nothing in it, but if I'm right, Sadie's in danger.'

'Sadie?' Verity looked bemused. 'What has she …?'

'It's too complicated to explain everything now, but I think she's discovered something about Peggy's father that Peggy desperately wants to keep a secret. She's taken Sadie home with her and I'm very concerned about it.'

'Sadie's in danger from Peggy?'

'Not Peggy, her father.'

'What's her father got to do with it?' Verity looked more bewildered than ever. 'What have you found out? Have you told the police?'

'I spoke to Chief Inspector Harris, but I don't think he took me seriously.'

'How can I help?' Colour had returned to Verity's cheeks and her hands had stopped trembling.

'First of all, do you know anything about Peggy's father? Has he been staying with her recently?'

'I've no idea. I know nothing about her family.'

'Do you know where she lives?'

'In Weatherton, I think. I expect her address'll be in the staff file.'

Melissa was on her feet. 'Can we go and check?'

'I'm not exactly sure where to find it. It'll be just as quick to look in here.' Verity had already picked up the telephone directory and was flipping through it. She found the page and ran a finger down the names 'Peggy's short for Margaret so it'll be under Drage, M. – here we are. Bryony Cottage, Weatherton.'

'Which direction is that from here?'

'It's on the Cirencester Road.'

The opposite direction to Uphanger village. So Peggy wasn't giving Sadie a lift home, she was taking her to her own place. It was becoming more serious with every second. 'Verity, do you know the village? Could you find the cottage easily?'

Verity shook her head. 'I've got a feeling it isn't in the village itself – I once heard Peggy say her place was rather isolated. Why? Are you going there?'

'Yes.' Melissa jumped from her chair. At the door, another thought struck her. 'Did you notice if there are any other Drages in the book?'

'There's only one – the Honourable Mrs K.'

'Is that all?'

'Look for yourself. Why do you ask?'

'I just wondered if Peggy's father lives in the county.'

'Even if he does, his name won't be Drage.'

'What?'

'Peggy got divorced while she was working at Headwaters, but she kept her married name.'

'And you've no idea what her maiden name was?'

'Sorry.'

'Hm. Not much mileage in that direction.'

'Before you go haring off to Weatherton,' said Verity, 'Why don't I check whether Sadie's reached home yet, or left a message?'

'Good idea. You do that while I go and get my car keys.'

'She's not on the phone at home, but Mrs Lucas lives a couple of doors away. I'll ask her to pop round.'

'Don't say anything to frighten anyone. We still don't know for certain …'

'Don't worry.' Presented with something practical to do, Verity had thrown off her lethargy and despair.

Melissa hurried across the courtyard and fetched her coat, gloves and handbag. When she returned to the kitchen, Verity was just putting down the telephone. Her expression was serious as she said, 'Sadie isn't home yet, but no one seems especially concerned. Her mother told Mrs Lucas she often takes her time.'

'That settles it. I'm going to Weatherton. Verity, will you call Chief Inspector Harris right away on this number and ask him to send someone to meet me at Bryony Cottage. Tell him I said it's urgent ... *very* urgent.' Before she was out of the door, Verity was tapping out the number Melissa had scribbled on an envelope.

Thank God for someone who's quick on the uptake and doesn't ask too many questions, thought Melissa. She hurried back to the car park and set off in the direction Peggy had taken. A short distance along the Cirencester road, she spotted a sign indicating that Weatherton was five miles away.

When she got there, the village shop was just closing and she had to rap on the glass door to attract the attention of the proprietor, a cheerful-looking, rosy-cheeked dumpling of a woman. Precious minutes were lost as – following advice handed out by the Neighbourhood Watch Committee, she explained several times and at considerable length – the woman asked who she was and who she was looking for, and then came out of the shop and took a close look at her car before giving directions to Bryony Cottage.

It was only a short distance, but the lane was narrow and twisty; several times Melissa had to pull in close to the bank to edge past a car coming in the opposite direction. The cottage turned out to be a bungalow, set back behind a tall, close-clipped hedge of false cypress. The name was carved on a slab of lichen-covered stone propped against the gatepost; the gate itself stood open. Melissa drove on a few yards, found a convenient place where the grass verge was flat and wide, and parked.

There had been no sign of Peggy's white car on the gravelled drive. Perhaps she was not yet home. Perhaps she had taken Sadie somewhere else. But where? To a restaurant for supper, perhaps? For a moment, Melissa's sense of purpose became blurred under a fog of confusion and doubt. Was she, after all, making a complete fool of herself, adding a charge of wasting police time to that of withholding information?

Now she was here, she might as well check. Having thought up what she hoped was a plausible excuse for calling, she walked back and rang Peggy's doorbell. There was no answer. She rang again and rattled the letter-box. Still no sound. Determined to do the job properly, she followed the narrow flagged path that led behind the bungalow and knocked on the back door. She peered through all the windows, uncertain what she expected to see but determined to make sure. There was no doubt; the place was empty.

If her message had got through, the police should be here by now, but there was no sign of them. Maybe they hadn't been able to contact Ken Harris and no one else had considered it worth following up. She was on her own, without a clue what to do or where to go next. She stood in the driveway to the cottage, her hands in her pockets, and racked her brains. Just what could Sadie have discovered that Peggy would be anxious to conceal?

And then her brain made a quantum leap. Why on earth hadn't it occurred to her before? She hared back to the car, started it up, slammed it into reverse, backed up to the open gateway of Bryony Cottage and turned round. She remembered seeing a public call-box in the village. 'Please, God,' she muttered as she drove back – much too fast, but mercifully she met nothing on the way – 'don't let it be occupied, don't let it be vandalised, *please*!'

The call-box was free and in working order. Her fingers felt all thumbs as she scrabbled in her purse for change, fed it into the machine and tapped out Verity's number. 'Come on,' she muttered aloud. 'Answer *quickly!*'

It took six rings, and it seemed a lifetime. 'It's Melissa,' she said, and rushed on before Verity had a chance to speak. 'Don't ask questions, just do as I say. I need another address … get the phone book.' She stood with a pencil poised over a notebook, gnawing her lips, shifting her weight from one foot to the other, listening to the sound of rustling pages and mumbled names, while the seconds ticked away.

At last Verity came back to the phone; Melissa's hand trembled as she scribbled the details down. 'Right,' she said. 'Now call the police again and tell them that's where I'll be. And tell them to *hurry!*'

The address was in Cirencester. Thank God, she was already on the right road. Thank God, too, that she carried with her a book of maps of local towns. Back in the car, she grabbed it from the glove compartment and hunted frantically through the pages. When at last she located Mead Close it was a relief to find that at least it was on this side of town and easy to reach. Murmuring another fervent prayer, this time of supplication that she would not be too late, that her message to Harris would get through and that he would take it seriously, she threw the book aside and set off, driving like a demon until she saw ahead of her the graceful tower of Cirencester parish church.

It was almost seven o'clock. The little town basked in the glow of the setting sun, which was turning the western sky into an inferno of red and orange. There was no one about but a man and his dog walking along the footpath with long shadows at their feet; a few fallen leaves, early casualties of autumn, lay in bronze drifts at the roadside. There was very little traffic; most people would be at home after their day's work, preparing their evening meal, studying the paper to see what was on the television. As the light faded, they would draw their curtains and settle down, never dreaming that somewhere close by, next door maybe, a young girl's life was on the line.

She found the house; her stomach contracted at the sight of Peggy's car on the drive. She parked outside so that the police would see it immediately when they came ... If they came ... but they *must* come. If they didn't, it might mean curtains, not only for Sadie, but for Melissa Craig as well.

CHAPTER TWENTY-TWO

There was a long interval before Melissa's ring brought any response. As she waited in the glazed porch, subconsciously noting the external signs of middle-class respectability – a shiny brass coach lamp, pots of well-tended geraniums, a plastic milk holder containing a scrupulously clean, empty bottle, its pointer set at one pint – she could almost feel the tension inside the house, the reluctance on the part of the occupants to reveal their presence. She imagined their frantic, whispered consultations: *It might be a neighbour just calling round for something, or a door-to-door salesman. With the car on the drive, they'll guess someone's at home. They'll remember later if no one answers. You go. Say I'm out, you don't know when I'll be back. Say anything, only get rid of them … quickly.*

It was Peggy who at last came and cautiously opened the door; at the sight of Melissa, her eyes widened until they seemed ready to leap from her pale, startled face.

'You? What do you want?' she croaked.

'I want to talk to Sadie,' said Melissa, keeping her voice low, anxious not to be overheard by whoever might be lurking, invisible, in the background.

'S … Sadie?' Peggy licked her lips. Her eyes flickered and her head made a jerky movement, as if she had been about to glance behind her but checked herself just in time. 'What makes you think …?'

'I saw her drive away with you. She isn't at home and there's no one in at Bryony Cottage, so I think it's safe to assume you've brought her here.' Melissa's heart was racing and it was an effort to keep her voice steady as she went on, still speaking quietly, 'I'd like a word with her, please. Shall I wait here while you fetch her, or are you going to invite me in?'

With a helpless gesture, Peggy stood aside for Melissa to enter. As the door-latch clicked behind her, it sounded like a trap closing and she felt a surge of panic. She fought it down as she and Peggy faced one another in the narrow hallway.

Peggy appeared to be trying to speak, but no words came from her dry lips. Again, there was that involuntary movement of the head, almost like a nervous tic. In the momentary silence, Melissa thought she heard the creak of a door and the panic rose again like an advancing tide. What she had done was madness; she should have waited until the police came instead of venturing in here alone, but it was too late now. All she could do was play for time.

'Shall I wait here while you fetch Sadie?' she said again, and this time she could not entirely control the tremor in her voice.

Peggy made one last effort to prevaricate. Speaking a little more loudly, she said, 'I tell you, Sadie isn't here. I can't understand what makes you think ...'

'That's not true, is it Pegsy?' A man, speaking in an unnaturally high-pitched voice like someone remonstrating with a child, materialised from a doorway at the end of the passage. 'What has Daddy told you about telling stories?'

As her eyes went from his face to what he was holding in his right hand, Chandler's classic comment, many times quoted by aficionados of crime fiction, came into Melissa's head: *If you can't think what to do next, have a man enter with a gun in his hand.* In her overwrought state, the timing seemed almost comic. She felt an insane impulse to laugh. It must have shown for a moment, for he said, in the same infantile voice, 'Your friend likes my toy, Pegsy. My little Pegsy doesn't like me playing with it because it goes

bang.' Now he was addressing Melissa, confidingly, indulgently, a
fond parent excusing a little girl's irrational fears to an older, more
sensible child. 'You don't mind bangs, do you? This one doesn't
make a very loud bang anyway – would you like to hear it?' He
pretended to aim at the ceiling and Peggy gave a thin shriek and
put her hands over her ears. 'No Daddy, don't do that!' she begged.

He lowered the gun, smiling with closed lips. 'Daddy was only
teasing. Bring your little friend in here, Pegsy.' He gestured towards
the room he had just left.

Peggy made feeble movements with her hands. 'You know I'm
frightened of toys that go bang, Daddy,' she whimpered. 'Promise
not to make it go bang.'

For a sickening moment, Melissa thought Peggy was as mad
as her father; then she saw her eyes, glazed with terror, and knew
that she was merely joining in the macabre game to humour him.
She was staring first at the gun and then at his face, her mouth
half open. Then she took a step forward and reached out a hand.
'Let Pegsy put it back in the toy-box, Daddy.'

He backed away, holding the gun out of reach, and wagged
a finger at her. 'Naughty, naughty, mustn't snatch from Daddy.'

'Nice Daddy, put it down and go get Pegsy a drinkie, *please*.' On
the last word, the childish intonation became a despairing groan.

'You can have a drinkie later. First you must do as Daddy says.
Come along now, both of you.' A harsh undertone crept into the
infantile wheedling. He moved away from the doorway, beckoning
like a policeman directing a line of traffic.

'Play along with him, for Heaven's sake,' said Peggy under her
breath as, reluctantly, she and Melissa entered the room ahead of
him. 'If you upset him, there's no telling what ...'

Melissa did not hear the end of the remark. Her eyes had gone
straight to a couch where Sadie, her mouth sealed and her hands and
feet bound with plastic tape, lay curled up with her knees against

her chest like an infant in the womb. Her eyes rolled wildly when she saw Melissa and she gave a faint, muffled moan.

'Keep quiet!' The voice was no longer soft and coaxing, but harsh and gritty; now there was a different kind of madness in the face of the man holding the gun. He made a threatening gesture with it; Sadie closed her eyes and buried her face in the cushions.

'It's all right, Sadie, he's only playing,' said Melissa. 'It's just a game, you see. I don't think it's a very nice game, though. Pegsy doesn't like this game, do you Pegsy? Ask Daddy to play something different.'

'Shut up. Sit over there.'

Plainly, that line wasn't going to work; she'd have to think of something else. The gun indicated a chair in the far corner of the room and then swung back, pointing directly at her. Fear drew a black curtain over her brain so that for a moment she was aware of nothing, could look at nothing but the weapon aimed at her heart. Then, with an effort, she shifted her gaze and met the eyes of the man who held it. It might have been her imagination, but she sensed that he was uncomfortable under her scrutiny, as if it made him less sure of himself.

Did that make him more, or less, dangerous? There was no doubt that he was seriously disturbed and therefore unpredictable, but she had heard many accounts of skilled negotiators persuading people like him into peaceful surrender. Without training, without any previous experience, she would have to try, play it by ear, make it up as she went along. Her life and Sadie's depended on it.

A moment ago she had been quaking; suddenly, she felt ice-cool, as if someone outside had taken charge of her brain and her reactions, someone who knew how to handle the situation and would talk her through it. It came as a surprise to hear herself saying, 'I think I'll stay where I am, if it's all the same to you.'

He looked taken aback, then shrugged and said, 'Please yourself. It makes no difference to us. Pegsy, fetch the other roll of tape.'

At the thought of being trussed up like poor Sadie, Melissa had a struggle to keep her appearance of calm. Inwardly she was cringing with horror, but there was nothing she could do but follow the line she had embarked on.

'We shan't be wanting the tape just yet, Pegsy – I want to talk to your Daddy a bit longer.' Once again, she forced herself to look him straight in the eyes. 'You've been so clever, making that effigy, writing the poems to read like haiku. Did you know your Daddy was a poet, Peggy?' she asked over her shoulder. 'When did you first learn what he was up to? You didn't know yesterday afternoon, did you? You wanted to help find Stewart's killer, which was why you agreed to answer my questions about Kate, even though it didn't show him in a very good light. You wouldn't have been so ready to talk if you'd known the truth.'

There was no reply, only faint sounds of tremulous, half-stifled weeping.

'I suppose the "Death of Hope" figure was meant to throw more suspicion on Maurice Dunmow, so the police would think it represented his sister?' Melissa continued. The murderer nodded, smirking. 'That was *very* clever!' she said.

'Yes, wasn't it?' The gun was still levelled at her and his gaze had not wavered, but he seemed pleased at the compliment. Was she getting through to him? *Keep it up, Mel, play for time – and Ken, for God's sake get here soon!*

'Brilliant, in fact,' she went on. 'And the coded link between "hope" and "Haughan" was neat as well – except that it was one of the things that put me on to you.'

'*One* of the things? What else was there?' Now his curiosity was aroused; she must spin this one out for all it was worth.

'Well now.' She glanced at the ceiling in the manner of someone trying to remember titles of books, or the names of people met at a party. 'There were several, only it took a little while to fit them all together. The first was the business of the German word *hoffen,* meaning hope, sounding the same as the name Haughan, plus Peggy knowing German and her father having been in the army in Germany. It wasn't much of a clue, but it was a start.'

'You figured out I was her father, just from that?' He sounded incredulous – but intrigued as well. She *was* getting through.

'Not straight away,' she continued. 'I only knew for certain when I got here. Up to then, it had been largely guesswork, although there were other clues.'

'It's a pity for your own sake you didn't stick to the ones in your books,' he sneered. 'Such a pity, too, that you won't be writing any more.' There was a pause, during which his eyes flickered and his lips moved silently, as if he was holding some kind of internal discussion. Then he said, 'What other clues?'

Curiosity had got the better of him again … but for how long? *For God's sake, Ken Harris, where are you?*

Aloud, she repeated, 'There were several. Do you know, I think I will sit down, if you don't mind.' She settled herself on a straight chair with its back to the wall, midway between Peggy and the man with the gun. The adrenalin was really going now; almost, she was beginning to enjoy herself, to forget this was a grim game of life and death. Almost …

'I just had this feeling there was something I'd missed,' she went on. 'You know how it is …'

'Get to the point!' he snarled.

Now he was losing patience. She'd been pushing her luck, getting too cocky. 'It was something I remembered hearing the day I came to Uphanger,' she said hurriedly. *Was it only the day before yesterday? It feels like a lifetime.*

'What was that?'

'You and Peggy were talking about Maurice Dunmow's sister Kate, who worked at Uphanger eighteen months or so ago. You said something like "the girl you told me about".'

'What of it?'

'Peggy is a very loyal employee; she was reluctant to tell me Kate's story, even when I questioned her about it. After all, it didn't reflect very well on Stewart. She agreed to talk only when I suggested it might help us find his murderer. Was it likely she'd go blabbing to a comparative stranger who'd only worked at Uphanger for a couple of months? But she might have confided in someone about it at the time ... someone she thought she could trust ... her father, for example.'

'More guesswork?' His laugh was scornful, but she could tell that he was disconcerted.

'*Inspired* guesswork, wouldn't you say? And then there was Sadie, who'd "taken a peek" at something she wasn't supposed to see, and learned something interesting about Peggy *or her father* – "speaking of her Dad", she said. She was just going to tell me when Peggy came back. I tried to figure out what it could have been. Then I remembered Peggy had been to collect tickets from a travel agent, for a holiday in the Canaries. For that, she'd need her passport. I thought, I'll bet Sadie couldn't resist taking that passport out of Peggy's handbag when her back was turned, to have a look at the photo. Passport photos are always good for a laugh, aren't they? I know mine is, I look ...'

'I'll give you just thirty seconds to tell the rest of it.' There was a rasp in his voice that sent a shiver down Melissa's spine. The sands were running out, there was no sign of the police, at any second his fragile control would snap.

'I believe that Sadie found something else in Peggy's handbag that she shouldn't have seen ... a letter in your handwriting, for example, or maybe a photograph of the two of you together. Which was it, Peggy?'

'A card with the name and address of my next of kin. I always keep it in my passport, just in case ...' Peggy's voice was a shaky, barely audible whisper.

'That's enough! Peggy, get that tape, stop her mouth and tie her up. I've got her covered. You, lie down on the floor.' He made a menacing gesture at Melissa with the gun. 'Any more fancy talk and I'll shut you up for good.'

Slowly, on legs that threatened to buckle under her, Melissa got to her feet.

'We have to do as he says,' Peggy whimpered. 'If we don't, he'll kill you – both of you.'

'He means to do that anyway – or didn't he tell you?'

Sadie gave another stifled moan. The gun swivelled menacingly from Melissa to the couch and back again.

'She's right,' he snapped. 'Better play it my way.'

'Oh no.' Melissa's courage had been oozing away, but she made one more despairing effort. She managed to remain upright, but her control was going; she could feel herself swaying and her voice rising in pitch as she gabbled on, 'You won't shoot us in the house. A neighbour's sure to hear and tell the police when our bodies are found. They will be found, no matter how cleverly you hide them. There'll be a search, when we're reported missing …'

'Shut up!'

'You want to get us as far away as possible before you kill us, don't you? Because you know you'd never get away with it if you did it here. But the game's up, because the police will be here any minute. You'll go to prison for a long, long, time, the rest of your life, maybe … and who'll look after Pegsy then?'

The effect of the final words was extraordinary. He gave a strangled sob; tears spurted from his eyes and ran down the furrows at the side of his nose.

'But I did it for her,' he said brokenly. 'She was all I had when her mother died. I dreamed of her finding a husband and being happy. She'd never be happy so long as that animal walked the earth and kept his hold over her. I wanted her to have children …

lots of children … and he made her destroy the only one she'll ever conceive … the doctor told us, because of that, there'll never be any more. That's when I gave up dreaming of grandchildren and began to dream of murder.' His voice became steadier as he told his simple tale of justifiable vengeance.

'And what about Maurice Dunmow, who was going to take the blame for what you did … and Ben Strickland? He didn't deserve to die, did he?'

'I had to kill him. I was afraid he'd recognise me – we were together on an army exercise years ago. When it got out how Haughan was killed, he might have remembered and told the police I'd trained with the SAS and they'd have started questioning me. I daren't take the risk. I couldn't let myself be caught, because Pegsy needs me. But it's all gone wrong. I'm no good to her now.'

He brushed away the tears with the back of his left hand and stared down at the gun that throughout his outburst had remained levelled at Melissa. He was on a knife-edge; it could go either way.

It was time to play the game again. 'Pegsy loves her Daddy very much,' said Melissa gently, 'and Daddy's done enough to prove that he loves her, so put the gun back in the toy box and we'll think of something else to play.'

For a moment, she thought she had won. Slowly, agonisingly slowly, he lowered the gun. Little by little, inch by inch, it moved towards the floor, while three frightened women held their breath and the tick of the clock on the mantelpiece seemed to grow louder and louder, like an instrument in an orchestra working up to the final crescendo. Then, without the slightest warning, his right hand swept up in an arc towards his own temple.

'Daddy, no!' Peggy screamed and hurled herself at him, seizing his arm, clawing at the hand that held the gun. Melissa dived forward to help, but she was too late; there was a bang and a scream of pain followed by a thud as Peggy crumpled to the floor. With a dismal cry, like the howl of a wounded animal, George Ballard dropped his weapon and sank to his knees, sobbing and babbling endearments as he cradled his child, trying with his bare hand to staunch the blood flowing from her breast.

As Melissa grabbed the phone and frantically punched out 999, there came sounds of violent knocking and shouts of 'Police, open up!' followed by a crash as the front door burst open and the room filled with men in blue. The blue tide was everywhere; it swept over her, swamped her, drowned her. Almost unnoticed in the confusion, she sank beneath the waves into darkness.

CHAPTER TWENTY-THREE

A chastened Melissa Craig sat drinking coffee in front of the fire in the sitting-room of Elder Cottage. For at least the fourth time within half an hour, Iris asked her if she was all right.

'I'm fine, Iris. Don't fuss, there's a dear. And thanks again for coming to fetch me.'

'No trouble. Nearly had a fit when PC Plod called from the hospital, though. Sounded pretty frantic.'

'All I did was pass out for a few moments. Anyone would think I was the one who got shot.'

'D'you feel well enough to talk?'

'Of course. I'm sure you're bursting to know the gory details, so ask away.'

'Will Peggy What's-her-name be okay?'

'I think so. I heard one of the medics say "No need to take her to the ITU", so she can't be that badly hurt.'

'What about the girl?'

'Sadie? She'll probably have nightmares for a while, poor kid. She'll need counselling, but she's young, she'll get over it.'

'Teach her not to poke her nose in, won't it? What about Verity and Maurice – you reckon they'll live happily ever after?'

'Time will tell. That's one load off my mind, Iris, knowing it wasn't Maurice who killed Ben. I really thought I'd have to live with that awful guilt for the rest of my life.'

'Let it be a lesson to you as well. Done your share of nosing in your time!' Iris reached out to caress Binkie, who was happily toasting himself at the hearth. 'I suppose,' she went on thoughtfully, 'Peggy's Dad will end up in the funny farm.'

'Probably. Poor man, he must have gone through hell.'

'Don't waste your sympathy.' Iris got up from her seat on the floor to put another log on the fire. 'Can I get you anything? More coffee?'

'How about a snort of your elderberry wine, to give my morale a boost? I dread to think what Ken Harris is going to say to me.'

'He'll give you a good wigging, and serve you jolly well right,' said Iris severely. 'And the doctor said "No alcohol" so forget that. Mel, what possessed you to …'

'Please,' Melissa begged, 'Don't scold me. I didn't stop to think, I was just terrified that madman would do away with Sadie before the police got to him. I'm sure he meant to hide her in his car and take her somewhere isolated to kill her, and Peggy didn't look like doing anything to stop him. If I hadn't turned up when I did, he might have done just that.'

'So he winged his own daughter instead! Prime example of Murphy's law!' Iris gave an unfeeling cackle. 'When d'you suppose she found out?'

'Who can tell? Maybe she suspected early on, but didn't want to believe it. Maybe she only faced up to it when she realised Sadie had stumbled on their secret. I imagine what happened was that she rang him up to tell him, he panicked and told her to find some pretext to bring Sadie to his house.'

'So she must have had some idea what was going on. That means she knew she was taking a lamb to the slaughter?'

'I'd like to be charitable and believe she thought they were just going to talk Sadie into promising not to tell, but I'm afraid you're right.' Melissa stared into the fire, reluctant to believe any woman capable of conniving at such a deed.

'What'll happen to her now?'

'It depends on what story she tells … whether the police believe her … whether there's any evidence to bring a charge … I just don't know.'

'Hmm. Ballard played a pretty cunning game, by the sound of it.'

'I shouldn't be surprised, when the whole story comes out, to find that he'd been planning to kill Haughan from the day he began work at Uphanger, maybe when he first learned there was a part-time job going there. He'd soon have heard about the mysterious poems and seen an opportunity to exploit them. My guess is he sneaked into the caravan to type his own messages – they'll probably find his prints on Maurice Dunmow's typewriter.'

'So that's why the relationship was concealed from the outset.'

'If Haughan had known, he'd quite likely have refused to give George Ballard the job. Or he'd have taken him on and then given the two of them a hard time, just for the hell of it. Knowing what sort of a man he was, they probably decided it was better if he didn't know. Once George began laying his plans, and even more after the first murder, it became essential to conceal their relationship.'

'How come you tumbled to it?'

'Inspired guesswork,' said Melissa. 'I wasn't sure until I actually came face to face with George and heard him talking to Peggy in that awful, infantile voice …' Her mind flew back to the bizarre scene in the house in Mead Close and she gave a violent shudder. 'I'll tell you the whole story in a day or two, but I don't think I can face going over any more of it tonight.'

'Don't get upset, it can wait.' Iris's tone was unusually gentle.

There was the sound of a car slowing down at the end of the track leading to the cottages, then a flash of headlights through a chink in the curtains as it drew up outside. 'No prizes for guessing who that is,' said Iris, her eyes alight with good-humoured mischief. 'Looks as if you'll have to tell it tonight after all. Want me to ask him in?'

Melissa gave a sigh of resignation and got to her feet.

'No, I'll go home and face the music there. He can't eat me, and he can't book me either – I haven't broken the law.'

'Just scared the pants off him. Never mind, he'll forgive you … by the end of the evening.'

There was no mistaking the meaning behind Iris's sly grin. An electric charge ran through Melissa's body and her thoughts went racing ahead. 'I'm sure he will,' she said.

A LETTER FROM BETTY

Dear Reader

Thank you so much for taking the time to read *Murder in the Orchard*, I hope you enjoyed it! If you'd like to stay in touch with news about my future publications, then please sign up to my newsletter here:

www.bookouture.com/betty-rowlands

If you really loved the book and would like to spread the word to other readers, I'd be so grateful if you would leave a review. You can also follow my fan page on Facebook and Twitter via the links below.

All very best,
Betty

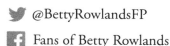 @BettyRowlandsFP
Fans of Betty Rowlands

Lightning Source UK Ltd.
Milton Keynes UK
UKHW010747220119
335989UK00011B/1140/P

9 781786 818737